NEVER TO FOREVER

BLUE RIDGE FALLS
BOOK 2

NOELLE STONE

CHAPTER ONE
MARIE

Smack.

Ding.

"Son of a bitch!" I hiss, rubbing the spot on my forehead where the coffee shop door just smacked me.

It's too early for this. I haven't had my coffee, and I'm not fully human yet. Not able to focus or have any real awareness of my surroundings, which is why I just tried to open the door with my face. Grumbling under my breath, I push the door open; the bell dinging again.

The scent of fresh coffee and pastries hits me as soon as I walk through the door, causing a sigh of relief to escape me. This is what I need to really get my day going.

Travis, the barista, looks up and smiles at me as I cross to the counter.

"Hey, Marie," he says, his brown eyes crinkling in the corners. "The usual?"

"Yes, please."

"Coming right up."

He turns to make my oat milk latte while I stand to the side and wait. Travis is a good kid, and he always gives me an extra pump of caramel because we bonded over his favorite fantasy book last year. I was able to get the complete series from the library, and as a result, I've earned free caramel for a lifetime.

While I wait, I dig my phone out of my pocket and check Instagram. The newest photo on my feed is of Haven, my best friend, holding a onesie in the air with a wide smile, announcing Baby Tallow's existence to the world. Her brown eyes sparkle and her auburn hair flows around her shoulders. The sight forces a smile to my lips. I honestly still can't believe that she's where she is right now.

Can't wait for our little one! Can't come soon enough.

"Marie! Your latte is ready!"

Blinking, I look up to find Travis holding up my to-go cup with a wide smile on his baby face. Tucking my phone back in my pocket, I make my way over to him to take the coffee.

"Thanks." Once the God's nectar hits my tastebuds, I moan in delight. "It's delicious, as always."

"Busy day?" He asks, his smile widening as he wipes the counters with a white rag.

"Nothing out of the ordinary. Heading to work, like every other morning."

He nods, looking genuinely interested in my answer, even though we have similar conversations most days when I stop in. I'm a creature of habit. On my walk to work as the local library's Associate Librarian, I always stop in for my latte, have a quick chat with Travis, and then continue on my way to the library.

"Has the new book in the *Dark Sorcerer Chronicles* arrived yet?" he asks eagerly.

"Not yet. It should be in this week. I'll let you know the moment it arrives, though."

"Thanks, Marie," he beams, excitement dancing in his eyes. I love when I see people get excited about books... especially young people. It gives me a warm, fuzzy feeling and makes me happy to walk into the library every day.

"Oh, shoot, look at the time," I quickly say, checking my watch. "I should get going. Don't want to be late. See you tomorrow!"

"See you, Marie!"

Strolling down the sidewalk, I enjoy my coffee and the calm before I get to work. The library is just off Main Street, so about a five-minute walk from the coffee shop. The sun gets higher and its warmth banishes away the morning chill. It won't get too much warmer even though it's Texas and the end of January, but it's still going to be a beautiful day.

Those feelings dip when I cross in front of the last building on the street. Pausing, I stare at the locked front doors and dark windows of the storefront. It's dark inside and slightly rundown, but there's an old-fashioned charm with carved details around the front door and windows that call to me.

There's so much potential here. It's easy to imagine walking inside to shelves of books and the smell of coffee. Having my latte in my hand is really helping me with the visualization. People would browse the bookshelves, trying to decide on a purchase. Other patrons would sit by the large front windows at little tables, sipping hot drinks. This bookstore would have a wide selection of all genres, and there would be other seating areas with cushioned chairs where people could sit, relax, and talk about what they're reading.

I'm filled with a mixture of longing and sadness as I stand there, imagining what this abandoned little shop could be... and what it used to be—a cute little boutique that sold women's clothing and was as good as a playground for a little girl. When it was my mom's store, the interior was painted white with brightly colored flowers all over the walls. Mom would bring me with her, and I would run around the place as long as I didn't bother the customers.

This used to be one of my favorite places in the world, but now it symbolizes my disappointments and shortcomings. I have so many plans and dreams for this place, but I've barely done anything to it since I took full possession at eighteen. After my mom died in a car accident when I was seven, I was told the store was put into a trust for me. Apparently, they didn't trust a child to own and operate a small business. When I turned eighteen and was old enough to fully take over, I planned on opening the bookshop that I'd been dreaming of since I was a teenager.

I mean, I never planned on leaving Blue Ridge Falls, anyway.

However, I guess life doesn't always give us what we want.

It's been nine years, and I'm no closer to opening my shop than I was at eighteen. Between my busy schedule and my student debt from my Master's program, I just haven't had the time or resources to make it happen.

Forcing my gaze away from the store, I turn and shuffle down the sidewalk, desperate to grab hold of the contentment I was experiencing right after the coffee shop. By the time I reach the library, I've had some success in bringing my mood back up. Yes, I wish I'd made more progress on the shop by now, but I've been busy. That doesn't mean I'll never have my shop... I just have to be more patient.

Reaching the library's front desk, I set my coffee down next to my computer and shrug out of my jacket. As I get settled, a figure steps out of the Employee Only area behind the front desk, catching my attention.

"Oh, good morning, Marie. How are you, dear?"

I smile up at Kathy, the head librarian for the Blue Ridge

Falls's public library. "Good morning, Kathy. I'm good. How about you?"

She waves her hand and shakes her head, looking irritated.

"Oh, I'd be so much better if the city council wasn't filled with idiots."

I fight to keep from smiling in amusement. There's nothing that can piss Kathy off faster than the town's city council. It's even funnier because she's usually such a kind, loving woman with the patience of a saint. She looks like a stereotypical librarian with a sweet, softly-wrinkled face and warm brown eyes. Her hair is even pulled back into a neat ballerina bun, and she wears silver spectacles, which are usually parched on the end of her nose. She's cute, approachable, and doesn't look like she's got a mean bone in her body... which she doesn't.

Unless you try to fuck with her library. Then she'll cut you.

"What'd they do this time?" I ask, plopping down in my chair. "Try to trim our budget again?"

"They wouldn't dare," Kathy growled. "No, no, nothing like that. They want to put a statue out front of the building... some explorer that had a hand in founding the town or some such nonsense."

That makes me chuckle. "A statue? You're pissed off about a statue?"

"Of course!" Kathy exclaims, hands on her hips. "Why should they choose the library, of all places, to put the statue in front of? What do we care about who founded this town? This is that Fred Wallace's doing, mark my words. He's still sore that I convinced the council to shut down his proposal of selling off half our collection to pay for new computers in city hall. As if such a thing makes any sense! That man goes out of his way to be a pain in my backside."

"Keep fighting the good fight, Kathy!" I cheer, knowing it doesn't really matter what I say right now. She's in library-protection mode, which means she might as well be the Terminator. Nothing will distract her from her mission.

To kill Fred Wallace... Well, his political career. Not Fred Wallace himself.

Probably.

"Thank you, dear." Kathy releases a long breath and then shakes her head. "I don't want to talk about that curmudgeon anymore."

"Then who will we talk about?" I tease, waiting for my computer to boot up.

She claps her hands together, "Oh! I know who. Garrett Young."

I instantly tense at the name and my heart drums harder against my ribcage.

"What about Garrett?" I don't bother hiding my blatant curiosity and excitement. Kathy is all too aware of my massive crush on Garrett Thomas Young.

"I saw him yesterday." Kathy waggles her eyebrows as she eyes me knowingly. "Such a handsome young man. Tall, dark, and my-oh-my, those green eyes of his! A girl could get lost gazing into them."

She gives me a wink and I can't help but chuckle.

"I'll win him over one way or another," I joke. "He can't resist this forever."

Running my hands down my sides, I wiggle a bit and give Kathy an exaggerated duck face. She laughs and I join her, though deep down, I feel a pang of longing thinking of Garrett. I've had feelings for him since I was eighteen, and I tried to ask him out when I was getting my Masters, thinking I was finally mature enough for him and that our age gap didn't matter anymore, but he turned me down. It hurt so bad, and I was so embarrassed, I never asked him again... but my feelings for him have only grown through the years.

Which is pretty pathetic if you ask me, but I can't help myself.

There's just something about those green eyes that make my heart race.

However, it's pretty clear Garrett has no interest in me and doesn't see me as more than Haven's best friend. I'm nothing but a kid in his eyes, and the ten-year age difference between us doesn't help that fact at all.

My thoughts are interrupted when my phone buzzes. I push all thoughts of Garrett out of my head and, seeing that it's my dad, answer the call.

"Hey, Dad."

"Marie, Meredith and I need you to watch Josie today," he says.

Ah. Yes, I should've guessed. Dad doesn't just call out of the blue to check in and see how I'm doing. He always needs something, or rather, my stepmother, Meredith, is making demands.

"Dad, I'm at work..."

"She can hang out in the kid's section. She'll be fine."

No actual discussion. No care of what I already have on my plate for the day. I wish I could say I'm surprised, but there's rarely any consideration of my life or schedule when a free babysitter is needed. I'm always tempted to say no when Dad and Meredith just shove their responsibilities onto me, but I don't. It's not my step-siblings' fault that our parents hoist them onto me whenever they want. I adore those kids, and I never want them to feel like an inconvenience or a burden.

And, I suppose, I have some sympathy for Dad and Meredith. Five kids is a lot, especially when several of them are under the age of ten. I can't really begrudge them the desire for help... I just wish they'd actually ask me instead of telling me I'm watching kids.

"All right, Dad." I sigh, shaking my head. "I'll look after her today."

"We'll be there in twenty."

Just like that, he hangs up the call. No goodbye, thank you, or show of affection or gratitude whatsoever.

Typical.

"Everything all right?" Kathy asks as I set my phone back down.

I force a smile as I look back up at her. "Yep, everything's fine. My Dad is just dropping Josie off soon. Is it okay if she hangs out? She'll mostly be in the children's section."

Kathy frowns at my question as if I need to even ask her. "Of course, it's okay. You know that."

"Thanks, I appreciate it."

Kathy stares at me, and I can practically hear the unspoken questions rattling around in her mind.

Why do you put up with this? Why don't you say no?

She doesn't ask the questions. She and I know what my answer would be—I love my family, especially my step-siblings, and I'll do just about anything to help them grow and learn and become their own people. I wish I'd had the same support growing up. To have someone in your corner who loves you unconditionally and wants you to meet your full potential is something a lot of people take for granted.

I lost my person when I lost my mom, and then again when Leilah died. Which has made me more determined when it comes to my siblings. I refuse to let any of them ever feel that level of loneliness.

Turning to my computer, I get started on my work for the day. No use lingering on dreams and what-ifs—the here and now demand my full attention.

CHAPTER TWO
GARRETT

Carson's is surprisingly busy this evening. Usually, on a weekday, there might be a handful of people spread out throughout the bar, relaxing after a long day of work or drowning their sorrows. Tonight, a small crowd gathers at the far end of the bar. I don't recognize any of the men or women standing together, drinking cocktails and chatting. They're all dressed in business wear—dresses, pencil skirts, shirts, ties, and slacks. They don't look like the typical Blue Ridge Falls blue-collar crowd.

"Need another, Garrett?" the bartender, Carl, asks, pulling my attention away from the crowd of pencil pushers. He's pointing at my empty beer bottle and gazing at me with a cocked brow.

"Yeah," I tell him. "One more."

He goes to grab me a fresh beer, and just as he brings it over to me, the bar's front door opens. A tall figure in a gray suit with styled brown hair comes strolling inside. He looks around, and when his familiar blue eyes land on me, he grins and makes his way over to me.

"I see you started without me," he says, settling onto the stool next to mine.

"Wanted to get your tab warmed up for you," I tease, lifting my new beer to my lips before taking a swig. "What's the point of being best friends with Christian Tallow if I can't get a few free beers now and then?"

Christian chuckles and waves a hand at Carl.

"I'll have the same as him," Christian says, pointing to my beer. Carl goes off to grab another and Christian looks back at me. "I suppose I can't blame you then. Glad to hear that my label as best friend supersedes brother-in-law, though."

"I knew you first. You were my friend before Haven's husband, so I take precedence."

Christian raises his bottle and clinks it against mine. "If you say so."

"How is Haven?" I ask, as we both take a drink. "You guys had a doctor's appointment today, didn't you?"

"We did." Christian nods, the corner of his mouth quirking up. "It went well. Everything with the baby is good. It's healthy and growing and everything is right on track. Haven's feeling great and the doctor says she's in perfect shape."

I smile softly. "That's good. I'm glad it's all going well."

As excited as I am for my sister's pregnancy, I'm also nervous, but I'd never say so out loud. Since Mom died, we don't have any family left except for each other and our stepfather, Peter. Pregnancy comes with risks, and the thought of losing her terrifies me. Though, I'd never tell her or Christian this. They've got enough to worry about getting ready for the baby on top of taking care of Oliver, Christian's son from a previous relationship.

"I'm sure that's got to put your mind at ease," I say.

"Yeah, it does. When Theresa was pregnant with Oliver, I was nervous for her, of course, but my focus was entirely on the baby. With Haven, it's different. I just love her so fucking much. She keeps telling me I'm hovering, but I don't want to let her out of my sight. I tried to convince her to hire full-time house staff so she's never by herself when I'm gone, but she refuses, still insisting that having other people take care of her home all the time stresses her out."

I let out a snort of laughter, imagining Christian as a cartoon chicken, wearing an apron and running around bawking.

"I'm sure you're annoying the shit out of her," I reply with a chuckle, knowing exactly how my sister is.

"Sure am," Christian declares, tilting his chin. "Doesn't mean I'm going to stop."

"Of course not. I wouldn't expect anything less."

"Thankfully, we have you and Marie."

At the mention of Marie Green, every muscle in my body tenses. I've known her since we were kids, and she's as close to Haven as if the two were sisters. For a long time, I thought of her similarly, even though she's made it clear over the years that she carries a torch for me. Lately, I've been thinking of her completely differently. Especially after the night out she and Haven had before the wedding.

Carrying her around that dance floor was unlike anything I've ever felt before. And then when I walked her home, it took everything in me to not cross the line between us. It's hard not to notice how beautiful she is. She's not a little girl anymore but a gorgeous woman with dark brown hair that falls in waves down her back, dark brown eyes always filled with mischief. Her lightly tanned skin is smooth, and she has a spattering of freckles across her nose.

And her body... she's lean and fit, but she has soft curves around her hips, and her breasts look like they'd fit perfectly in my hands.

More than her looks is her personality. She's smart, funny,

sometimes blunt, but can be a goofy tomboy who's protective of the people she cares about most, including my sister.

"Yeah," I reply in a rough voice. I clear my throat before continuing. "Yeah, Marie's great."

"She is," Christian agrees, narrowing his eyes at me. "In fact, she's staying with Haven and Oliver tonight so I can go out to the oil fields."

I frown. "What? Why are you going out there? You're not supposed to go out there for another few weeks for the semi-monthly inspection."

Christian releases a long breath and takes another drink. "There's a problem with some machinery, and I have to go out there to see how to fix it. We don't have an engineer onsite at present because Joseph had an accident with the same piece of hardware and had to be taken into the hospital. I've got another engineer coming in from Dallas, but he won't be here for a few days, and in the meantime, the broken machine still needs fixing. Which leaves it up to me to head out there."

There's an uncomfortable heaviness in my gut at the thought of Christian away from Haven, working in the oil fields in a possibly risky situation. I know how much Haven will worry about him, and the thought of her stressed and anxious fills me with dread.

"Why don't I go for you instead?"

Both of Christian's brows shoot up. "What?"

"As a foreman, I know how to work the machinery almost as well as you do," I explain, with a smirk. "I can go out there and fix it, and you don't have to worry about it."

Christian blinks, seemingly caught off guard by my offer.

"Garrett, I appreciate the offer, but you don't have to do that. You just got back from the fields a few days ago, and it's your time off. I can handle it..."

"It's not a big deal," I reply, slapping Christian's shoulder.

"It's just a quick out and back, right?" With a chuckle, I add, "If it makes you feel better, you can just lend me your private jet, so the trip's even faster."

Despite my light tone, Christian appears hesitant.

"I don't want to put you out..."

I give his shoulder a squeeze.

"Christian, dude, you wouldn't be putting me out. I want to help, and I don't want my sister awake all night and stressed out about her husband's safety. You don't want that either."

He gazes at me in silent hesitation, but I can see the longing. It's clear he wants to say yes to my offer. He doesn't want to leave Haven behind when she might need him.

"Just say yes," I urge him. "We both know you want to, and we both know I'm more than capable of handling this."

The moment he gives in, relief floods his features, though he quickly tries to hide it. His shoulders relax and a soft smile twitches his lips as he nods.

"All right... if you're sure."

"I am. Trust me, it's going to be all right. You go home to your wife and Oliver, and I'll take care of everything else."

THE SKY IS pitch black by the time I make it to the oil fields. Even in the dark, the silhouettes of the heavy machinery tower over the rig. I barely caught a wink of sleep on the flight, but as soon as I step out of the truck that brings me from the private airfield Christian has for his jet, I'm in work mode.

"Garrett!" Mike, one of the night shift supervisors, calls out as he waves me over. "Glad you made it. We got a situation over by Drill Site Four."

He gives me a quick rundown as we walk toward the rig. The drill's been giving them problems, overheating, and acting up. They're trying to get through a tricky stretch, and it's been pushing the equipment harder than usual. It's not my first time handling a hiccup like this, but something about the way Mike's jaw clenches tells me it might be worse than he's letting on. I remember what Christian said about Joseph and his accident and a small ball of dread forms in my stomach.

When we reach the drill, the machinery looks like it's seen better days. There's a faint stench of burnt oil, and I can see spots where something's been leaking, a dark sheen against the dirt.

I pull my gloves tighter and nod to the other guys already on site. "Alright, let's get this beast back in line. Mike, kill the main power. Let's do this safely."

We all set to work, our flashlights casting sharp beams across metal and mud. I get down on my knees, checking the pipes and joints along the base. Pressure's building up in one of the hoses —it's hotter than it should be, and the last thing we need is for it to burst. I call for a wrench and get to loosening a few bolts to release the excess pressure.

But something doesn't feel right.

Rumbling, like the sound of thunder rolling just beneath my feet, vibrates under foot. I glance at Mike, who's looking around too, his face tense. He mutters under his breath and motions for us to step back.

The rumbling grows louder, and suddenly, chaos. The drill lets out a high-pitched whine. Before I can move, there's a sharp hiss—then an explosion. It's not huge, but it's powerful enough to throw me backward, and I land... hard.

My head slams against something solid—a wall, maybe. The pain is instant, bright white behind my eyes, and then everything blurs. The edges of my vision go dark as I try to get my bearings, my hand pressing against my head where it throbs like a hammer.

Voices are shouting, but the sounds are muffled, like I'm underwater. I blink, trying to focus, but my head feels as though it's filled with sand, weighing me down, dragging me into darkness.

I open my eyes one last time, glimpsing someone rushing toward me, yelling my name. Then the pain fades to numbness, and everything goes black.

CHAPTER THREE
MARIE

"Ugh, I can't wait until I'm done with this. What's the point of the SATs anymore, anyway? They're so outdated."

I look up and grin at Ally, my seventeen-year-old half-sister, who sits on the other side of my kitchen table. SAT study books are open and spread out in front of her, but Ally isn't looking at any of them. She's slumped in her chair, her chin resting in her hand as she scowls at me in obvious irritation.

"You're not wrong," I tell her, setting down the pen I've been using to score her latest practice test. "Unfortunately, colleges haven't figured that out yet... or they just refuse to move out of the dark ages. Either way, you want to get into a good school? You gotta play the game and nail these tests."

She groans, rolling her hazel eyes as she drops her head onto the table. Her long, chestnut-colored hair fans out around her, hiding her face completely. She's such a pretty girl—tall and slender, though she's complained to me more than once about her lack of curves. Of all my half-siblings, Ally and I are probably the closest. It helps that she's the oldest and I can relate to her better than the younger kids, but she's genuinely fun to have around. She's sarcastic, funny, and incredibly smart. Like a typical teenager, even if she often questions her abilities and puts on a cool and collected front when she's feeling vulnerable. I remember what it was like to be a teenage girl, and so I'm a sympathetic ear she can turn to when she needs some guidance or support.

"This suuuuuucks," she groans.

"I know, but think of it this way—you get a stellar score the first time you test, and you won't have to take the SATs ever again."

She turns her head to look up at me from beneath the curtain of her hair.

"Your optimism is annoying sometimes."

I wink at her. "You just don't want to admit that I'm right."

"Whatever," she grumbles as she sits back up. Picking up her pencil, she pulls one of her workbooks closer to her with a heavy, dramatic sigh.

Chuckling, I turn my attention back to her practice test, but before I can get through the next answer, my phone rings.

It's Haven calling. Huh, that's weird. It's late, and she's been so exhausted lately because of her pregnancy she's usually in bed earlier than this.

"Hey, lady. What's up?" I say into the phone as I answer.

"Marie, there's been an accident!" Haven exclaims, her voice panicked and fearful.

I tense, my heart hammering in my chest. "What happened? Are you okay?"

Ally looks up at me with a furrowed brow and a confused frown. I can tell she wants to know what's going on, but I hold up my finger to tell her to wait and not say anything yet.

"No, I'm fine," Haven replies, though she doesn't sound fine at all. "It's Garrett! He was out in the oil fields and there was some sort of explosion... I'm not sure... he's being flown to the St. Joseph's Medical Center in Houston..."

She dissolves into sobs, and I feel as if the floor has been ripped out from under me. Garrett's hurt?

"I'll meet you there," I declare, instinct taking over.

"Marie... I'm so scared..."

"Don't worry," I say, trying to sound calm and confident, even though that's as far from the truth as possible. Not at all. I'm terrified, and not knowing the extent of Garrett's injuries only makes it worse. I need to get to him and see him. Lay my eyes on him and make sure for myself that he's alive and okay... or that he's not.

Oh, god... what if he's not?

"Garrett is strong," I continue, forcing myself to stay above the panic so I can reassure Haven. "He'll be alright. I'll meet you at the hospital. Just breathe, okay?"

"I can't lose him..."

"You won't." My voice is sharper than I intend it to be. I can't let her finish that thought. It's just not an option. Garrett has to be okay because if he's not... "You won't lose him. Don't think like that. Just focus on one thing at a time. First, get to the hospital, and we'll find out his condition. Then, we'll go from there. Is Christian with you? Can he take you?"

"Yes... yes, he's going to drive," Haven whimpers. "I'll see you soon."

She hangs up, and the phone slips from my numb fingers, clattering on the table.

"Marie? What's going on?"

I blink, looking up and meeting Ally's worried gaze.

"It's... it's Garrett," I say. "There's been an accident..."

"Oh, my god!" Ally jumps up from her chair. "What are we waiting for? Let's get going."

She rushes around the table and grabs my arm, yanking me out of my chair.

"Don't worry," she says. "I'll drive."

A COUPLE OF HOURS LATER, when Ally and I get to the hospital in Houston, Haven is already there, along with Christian, Peter, and Oliver. They're gathered in a waiting area inside the emergency room. Haven is sitting in an uncomfortable-looking chair, her head in her hands, crying. Christian is next to her, his arm around her shoulders, and Peter is trying to keep Oliver distracted. The little boy is the spitting image of his dad with big blue eyes and dark brown hair, and that bright gaze is locked on Haven. He's clearly distraught by her fear.

Before I can say a word, Ally jumps into action. She hurries to four-year-old Oliver and kneels down in front of him. Ally has babysat Oliver before, so he doesn't shrink away from her.

"Hey, big guy," she says with a wide smile. "Do you want to go with me and get ice cream in the cafeteria?"

He blinks up at her but slowly nods.

"Okay." Ally offers him her hand, and he takes it. She leads him away, giving me a jerk of her chin as she passes by.

"Thank you, Ally," Christian calls after them.

Once Ally and Oliver are out of sight, I move to sit on Haven's other side. I feel like I'm shattering from the inside out, but I hold myself together as best I can. Haven is under enough stress as it is. She's only three months into her pregnancy, which means her risk of miscarriage is still high.

"Hey," I say softly, grabbing her hand. Haven immediately lifts her head and drops it against my shoulder.

I glance up at Peter. "How are you, Mr. Merritt?"

He gives me a shaky smile. I can't imagine what he must be going through right now—he lost his wife recently, and now his stepson is in the same hospital she died in, hurt and suffering.

"I'm all right," he tells me softly. He shoots Haven a quick look, his concern for her obvious. "We just need to pray that everything works out right now."

I struggle to swallow down my fear. Haven continues to cry, and I meet Christian's gaze over his sobbing wife.

"Have you heard anything yet?"

He shakes his head. "Not yet... other than he's alive. They're examining him now. A few other guys got caught in the explosion, but their injuries are minor compared to Garrett's, so they'll be okay. Garrett, unfortunately, was caught directly in the blast."

I swallow. "Okay, so we'll probably hear from the doctor soon?"

"I hope so," Christian murmurs, while I hold Haven in my arms. His phone suddenly rings and he pulls it out, frowning at the screen. "Give me a minute. I've got a team from the corporate office in Houston on the ground at the rig to oversee cleanup and repair. I've got to take this."

I nod, squeezing Haven closer to me. "Don't worry. I've got her."

He gives me a weary, grateful smile before turning and answering the phone, his voice trailing off as he walks away. "How the hell did this happen?"

It's another fifteen minutes before a doctor appears. Christian quickly hangs up his call. Haven and I stand up, and Peter moves to stand next to us.

"How is he?" Peter asks in a strained tone.

"Garrett's stable," the doctor says. "He's not in any danger, so you don't have to worry. There is a concussion, some cracked and bruised ribs, and his right shoulder blade is fractured. He should regain full use of his arm and full mobility, but he will have to spend at least a few weeks resting and recovering, and attend physical therapy. He'll be just fine."

The relief that washes over me is so intense, my knees shake.

Haven is clutching my arm, and I hold her just as tightly to stay upright myself.

"Can we see him?" Christian asks.

"Yes," the doctor nods. "He's down the hall. Room 104."

With that, he turns and walks away. Haven sags against me, and we hug. Thank God...Garrett's going to be okay. He's hurt, but he'll recover.

"Come on," Christian says. "Let's go see him."

The four of us move down the hallway to Room 104. The door is open, so we make our way inside. Garrett is lying in a hospital bed, his right arm fully wrapped in a stabilizing manner and his handsome face covered in bruises. My stomach twists, and I have to fight to maintain my composure. It's been so long since I've been in a hospital like this. My mom died in an accident, and every bit of that memory is slowly resurfacing as I stare at Garrett.

I hate seeing him like this—broken and in pain. He's always been so strong. So protective. He was the one who stepped up when his and Haven's mom got sick and took care of everyone. He sacrificed so much in order to keep his family together.

Garrett looks up at us as we enter and gives us a tired smile.

"Hey, guys," he says.

Haven rushes to him and takes his good hand. "Garrett! Oh, my God! I've been so worried."

"I'm okay," he assures her, pulling her in for a one-armed hug. "I promise, Haven."

Haven sinks into his embrace, and Garrett flinches. He keeps his pain contained, holding back so he doesn't upset Haven any more than she already is. Even if he hides it from everyone else, he can't hide it from me. I can read Garrett better than anyone because I've been crushing on him for so many years.

"Garrett, I'm so sorry this happened," Christian says,

running a hand through his hair as he shakes his head. "I should've just gone myself. This was my responsibility, and I..."

"If you had, it'd be you in this bed instead of me," Garrett tells him in a firm tone. "What would Haven do then? Oliver? The rest of the company? This isn't on you, man. I offered to go in your place and I'm glad I did."

"Fuck," Christian murmurs, his expression twisted with his guilt. "I'm going to take care of this, okay? The company will take responsibility for your treatments and anything else, and I'm going to figure out what the hell caused that machinery to blow like that."

Garrett gives him a reassuring nod. "I know you'll do right by me. We're good, I swear."

He looks up and meets my gaze. When he smiles, it's the same smile he gives to Haven. A brotherly one, and it makes my heart ache with disappointment.

"Hi, Marie," he says, waving me over.

I cross the room to stand by his bed. He takes my hand and squeezes it.

"Hey, big guy." I smile down at him. "Glad to see you're okay."

"I am," he assures me. "Thanks for looking out for Haven. I appreciate it."

I will always be there for Haven, but I wish Garrett would say he's just happy that I'm there because it's me. He only ever sees me as his sister or as Haven's best friend, nothing more, no matter how much I wish he would.

"No problem," I say, keeping my swirling thoughts to myself. Now's not the time. "You know I'd do anything for you guys."

Anything and more. These people are my family, as much as my father, stepmother, and siblings. Sometimes, it feels like more so.

About fifteen minutes later, Ally walks through the door with Oliver in her arms. His face nestled against her shoulder, but he perks up when he spots Garrett.

"Uncle Gary!" he exclaims, frowning as he looks Garrett over. "Are you going to be okay?"

Hearing Oliver call Garrett, Gary, makes me laugh. Only Garrett's mother ever called him Gary and the fact that Oliver calls him that now, is far too amusing.

Because he hates it.

Garrett gives him a reassuring smile, though I can see the pain in his eyes. "Don't worry about me, buddy. I'll be just fine."

Oliver doesn't look entirely convinced as he clings to Ally and eyes Garrett warily. This is clearly a lot for the little boy, seeing his uncle in this state.

Haven and Christian exchange a look. I can see that Haven is torn—stay with Garrett, or take Oliver home? Before she or Christian can say anything, I speak up.

"How about Ally and I take Oliver home and watch him tonight? That way you guys can stay here."

"Oh, Marie, you don't have to do that," Haven quickly protests. "It's okay, Christian and I..."

"It's not a problem," I insist. "Really. We'll just go and stay with him until you guys get home."

Haven hesitates, but I can tell she wants to say yes. She doesn't fight the urge for long and slowly nods.

"All right," she says. "I really, really appreciate it."

She moves in to give Oliver a hug and a kiss. "You be good for Ally and Marie, okay? Daddy and I will be home soon."

Oliver nods and glances toward Christian, who gives him a smile and steps closer so he can give the little boy a kiss on the top of his head as well.

"We'll see you soon, buddy. Goodnight."

"Goodnight," Oliver murmurs. Ally squeezes him to her

and he snuggles against her shoulder as he waves to his parents. Ally takes him out of the room and I move to Haven's side.

I give her a hug and then step back and look back down at Garrett. My throat tightens as I look at his black and blue face, and pressure builds up behind my eyes. I need to get out of here before I burst into tears.

"I'm really glad you're okay," I murmur, gazing into his eyes.

"Me too," he replies, his tone soft.

We stare at each other for several seconds, and there's so much I want to say to him. How scared I was when I first heard about his accident. How relieved I am that he's okay.

How much I feel for him.

I think back to when I first realized I was in love with him. It happened in an instant—I was eighteen and in a bad situation with a boy who didn't like to hear 'no,' and Garrett came swooping in to defend me. My white knight. I realized then that my feelings for him were more than friendly or sibling-like.

Maybe it's my imagination, but I feel like something passes between us as our gazes stay locked for longer than entirely necessary. Can he see everything I'm feeling right now? Or am I just being overly optimistic and hopeful?

He pulls his eyes from me, and I snap back to reality. No... I had to have imagined that. Garrett doesn't want me... not yet.

But maybe someday soon, he will.

CHAPTER FOUR
GARRETT

After five days in the hospital, I'm restless and ready to get the hell out of here. I'm still suffering from headaches and sensitivity to bright light, but I don't get dizzy every time I stand up, which is good because the doctor is finally comfortable letting me go home.

When he discharges me, I'm buzzing with eager energy to escape the confines of my hospital bed. He gives me a long list of precautions and rules for my recovery, but he could tell me I need to shave my balls and dip them in lemon juice every day and I'd agree if it got me out of here faster.

Christian and Haven arrive to pick me up, and when my sister walks through the door to my room, her eyes fill with tears. Before she hurries to me, wrapping me into a warm embrace. She's been doing that every time she's seen me since my accident.

"How are you feeling?" she asks, instantly going into mother hen mode. As she looks me over, as if looking for fresh injuries.

"I'm good," I assure her with a smile. "I promise. You don't have to worry about me."

She gives me an exasperated look that reminds me so much of our mom that my heart flips.

"Of course I'm going to worry," she insists. "You're my big brother, and I love you. I'm always going to worry about you, just like I worry about Christian and Oliver. You're my boys."

It's hard to argue with that, so I just give her a kiss on her forehead. "All right, I understand. Still, don't stress yourself out. Think of the baby."

"Oh, don't you get fussy over me." She sighs, waving her hand dismissively. "I'm fine."

"Don't want me to worry about you?" I tease. "Bit hypocritical of you, sis."

Haven rolls her eyes and huffs out a breath of frustration. "Don't be an ass. Let's get you to our house before I break your other arm."

"Your house? Why am I going to your house?"

She frowns up at me. "So we can take care of you. Duh."

I glance over at Christian with an arched brow. "She's joking, right?"

He shrugs before letting out a soft chuckle. "Afraid not, buddy. The wife wants you to come home with us so she can fuss over you, and what the wife wants, she gets."

Shit.

Haven gives me a smug look, and it's clear that there's no way I'm going to get out of this. "That's right—what the wife wants, the wife gets."

"I'm not a little kid, Haven. I can take care of myself."

"Weren't you just saying that I needed to think of my baby?" she says. "I'm doing just that. If you don't come home with us, it's going to stress me out. You don't want that, do you?"

That's a low blow.

Clenching my teeth, I fight down the frustration bubbling up inside me.

"Playing that card, huh?"

"Yeah, I am," she snaps. "Garrett, seriously, you have a fractured shoulder and a concussion. You're out of your mind if you think I'm going to leave you be alone right now. So, are you going to willingly come home with us, or am I moving in with you while you recover?"

I glance back at Christian, who looks startled.

"Woah, Haven, sweetheart," he says. "We didn't talk about you staying with Garrett..."

And I definitely don't want her in my house.

"Enough, already," I grumble. "I'll come home with you guys, okay? Everyone just relax."

Haven looks pleased at my acquiescence.

"Good choice," she grins. "Let's get going."

Gathering the few things I have with me, I drop into the wheelchair that's been brought for me and allow myself to be wheeled out of the building. Christian pulls up his truck, and after helping Haven inside, he moves to help me as well.

"Don't you dare," I growl, giving him a pointed look.

He puts up his hands in surrender. "You got it, buddy."

Easing into the backseat takes a moment. I'm awkward and clumsy when it comes to moving around because my arm and chest are both cast to keep my shoulder stable. But damn it, I'm determined to do it myself. I don't need to be babied. At least within the next two weeks, the doctor will hopefully remove the cast and get me into a sling instead.

That should make things easier.

As we drive to their sprawling acreage outside of town, I sit back and half-listen as Haven chats away in the front seat. She can fill the silence. That's no problem for me. I'm already tired and don't have the energy to be engaging or social. Plus, the sunlight stings, so I close my eyes. Once we get to their house, Haven walks me inside and ushers me into the living room.

"Sit down," she orders, pointing to the couch. "I'll go get you something to eat and drink. You must be starving after three days of hospital food."

I can't argue with that. "That sounds good. Thanks."

"Oliver will be at daycare for a few more hours, so we can get you settled before he comes in with his crazy toddler energy," she explains.

I chuckle at the thought of Oliver coming in with nothing but excitement as he tells everyone he sees about his day at daycare. The boy doesn't lack energy, that's for sure. "I look forward to his wild toddler energy."

She smiles and I can see the relief in her eyes before she turns and hurries off to the kitchen. That makes me feel a little better about being strong-armed into this arrangement. If it puts my sister's mind at ease, I can put up with a few days of babying, but just a few.

Haven will drive me batshit crazy if I let this go on for too long.

Christian comes into the room and settles into an armchair next to the couch.

Sighing, he looks at me. "Thanks for agreeing to stay here. Haven wasn't going to let the issue drop if you kept saying no."

"I'm aware," I snort. "I've been dealing with her stubborn ass a lot longer than you have, remember? She's a caretaker, though. She took on that role for our mom, and I don't suppose it's something she can give up on that easily."

"Yeah, that's a good point," Christian murmurs, glancing toward the door leading to the kitchen, where we can hear Haven busying herself with whatever she's cooking. "I've been working on convincing her that it's okay for people to take care of her now and then, but it's not an easy thing for her, sitting back and not taking care of everyone around her. Hell, even taking these few days off from work so she could be in Houston at the hospital with you has made her a little stir crazy."

It's one of my sister's best and worst qualities. She can be so selfless and caring, but she sometimes takes it too far and forgets about her own wellbeing. When Mom got sick, Haven dedicated pretty much her entire life to taking care of her and the rest of us. She insisted she didn't need a relationship of her own or a real life of her own—she was perfectly happy with her self-appointed role as caretaker. I'd always wanted more for her. A family of her own, someone to love and take care of her, and our mom wanted that too.

Thankfully, Haven met Christian, and though their relationship didn't start off as a love story (more a mutually-beneficial business arrangement), it ended that way. Was it difficult to wrap my head around my sister and best friend being together? Yes, yes, it was. Do I still cringe and want to throw up a little when they get lovey-dovey with each other? One hundred percent. But my sister is happy, and I know Christian adores her, and ultimately, that's what matters most.

"So," Christian continues, breaking through my runaway thoughts. "What are your plans now?"

"What do you mean?"

He shrugs a shoulder. "Do you still want to go back to working in the oil fields once you're healed up?"

The question catches me off guard a little.

"I, uh, haven't really thought about it."

Christian leans forward and rests his elbows on his knees.

He gives me a thoughtful look before saying, "I think you should take this time and think about what you really want to do."

I frown, confused. "You don't want me to go back to work?"

It's something I'd expect to hear from my friend, but Chris

tian is also technically my boss, so I'm kind of surprised by the suggestion.

"That's not it," he answers. "You're a damn good worker, and the company will definitely be worse off without you, but is it really what you want to do with your life?"

"Where's this coming from?" I ask with a frown, as I watch him glance towards the doorway of the kitchen before leaning closer to me.

"Haven told me that this isn't what you wanted to do with your life, Garett. You had dreams at one point in time."

I can't help the little scoff that leaves me as I shake my head. Of course, Haven would tell Christian about that kind of thing. "None of that matters, Christian. My dreams didn't pay the bills... the oil field does."

"Well," he says with a pause, his smile widening. "Lucky for you...you're going to be on disability for a while, and the company will be covering your medical bills and providing workers comp, so you don't have to worry about anything financially. You really could take this time to figure out what might be next for you. Of course, you don't have to. You can absolutely come back to work when you're better. I just want you to know that if you did want to do something else with your life, I'll support you"

"That's a brilliant idea! You could finish your degree!"

Christian and I both turn, surprised, to find Haven standing just inside the doorway of the room. She's holding a tray with a sandwich and sparkling water, her eyes wide and bright with excitement.

"My degree?"

She hurries over to me, setting the tray down on the coffee table before sitting next to me.

"You were so close to finishing," she says, grabbing my hand and squeezing it. "I know stepping away from school to help pay for Mom's medical bills and keep us all afloat was really hard for you, but now is your chance to go back and finish what you started!"

I nearly laugh at the idea. Me? Back in school?

"Haven, I'm thirty-seven." I shake my head. "Who goes back to school at my age, after so long? I'd look ridiculous hanging around all those twenty-something college students."

"You could do it online," she suggests. "You only need, what? One or two more classes to get your full credits? An English elective and a final finance class?" She suddenly gasps, her excitement doubling as some realization hits her. "You could study at the library and have Marie help you!"

At the mention of Marie's name, my heart races and my blood heats. I drop my gaze to try and hide it. I haven't seen Marie since my first night in the hospital. When she'd shown up, I'd been so happy to see her, it had caught me off guard. I did my best to act like I normally would around her because I didn't want to make things weird or awkward with everyone else around. She'd been so beautiful, her dark hair slightly mussed and cheeks pink, wearing black leggings that had shown off her shapely legs and perfect ass and, despite how much pain I'd been in, my cock stirred.

The memory floods me with guilt. I can't be having those types of thoughts—not about her. I made a promise, and there are some lines I just can't cross...

"That's not necessary," I insist. "Marie's a busy woman, and that's her place of work. I don't want to burden her—."

"You don't need to worry about that," Haven replies quickly. "She'll be able to help you with your English course, because, let's be honest, that was never your strong suit. She's already helping Ally with her college applications and SAT prep, so you could probably just hop in on their sessions together. I'm sure Ally won't mind. Besides, it's not like you're going to be able to type yourself, or even stare at a computer screen for long with your concussion. It'll be good just to have someone around to help you when you need it, and it'd be difficult for Christian and I to be available because of our jobs. It'll be easier for Marie. I'll give Marie a call and get everything arranged!"

She hops up with surprising agile for a pregnant woman and hurries out of the room before I can untie my tongue and object. Christian chuckles from his chair as I lean back slightly on the couch, turning my narrowed gaze to him.

"Shut up," I mumble. "Your wife is a crazy person."

"She's not wrong though."

I can't help but frown, as my gaze deepens. "No?"

"Why not finish your degree?" Christian leans back and crosses one leg over the other. "It was a finance degree, right? There'd be a place for you in the company with a degree like that. Higher up, administrative, better pay... I would seriously consider it if I were you."

I have to admit, that is some solid motivation. Not having to break my back on the oil rig—not having to spend weeks away from home at a time—it's definitely tempting.

"Fine... I'll think about it."

He smiles, satisfied with my response. "That's all I ask. Now, eat your sandwich and relax. I'll go try to rein in Haven."

"Good luck," I chuckle as he gets up to walk out of the room.

Alone, I think about Christian's offer more seriously and wonder if maybe this accident might have been a blessing in disguise. A chance to reset my life and do something more.

I mean, really, what do I have to lose?

<hr>

A COUPLE NIGHTS LATER, after Haven, Christian, and Oliver have turned in for the night, I'm left alone in the living room restless and not ready to go up to my own bed yet, the soft hum of the heater the only sound in the otherwise quiet house. My shoulder aches with a dull, persistent throb, and my head and neck are killing me, but I grit my teeth and ignore it. The pain reminds me I'm grounded here for a while, whether or not I like it. As much as I appreciate Haven's concern and her insistence on taking care of me, I've come to appreciate night time when I can actually have some real alone time.

I look around at the empty space; at Christian's bookshelves lined with titles about business, oil fields, and economics—subjects he's lived and breathed for years. He always made it look easy. Me? I was the one out there getting my hands dirty, fixing machines and working the rig. Christian was capable of doing all that too, and would often go out and get his hands as dirty as mine, but the main difference between us has always been that he doesn't have to do that. He doesn't have to work the rig himself. He could easily stay in his fancy office and delegate all that to other people. I don't have any choice—it's the only work I'm able to fall back on. Or, that's what I've believed for a long time now.

Am I really capable of more?

With a sigh, I open my laptop and pull up Google. "Online finance programs," I type with one hand, and hundreds of results flood the screen. It feels strange even considering this. It's been so long since I stepped away from school... can I really go back? What if it's too difficult and I fail?

What if I succeed?

I scroll through a few pages; the programs blurring together, the screen's brightness stinging my eyes. I turn it down, but still need to take breaks and look away from the screen often. Finally, I find a program that's practical, fully online, and has decent reviews. There's a flexible schedule too, which means I could fit it in around my physical therapy sessions. I click on the

"Apply Now" button and start filling out the form. My fingers hesitate on the keys a few times, like my brain can't keep up with what I'm doing. Name, contact information, previous education—all pretty standard stuff. When I get to the section that asks about why I'm applying, I pause. The empty box seems to stare back at me, waiting for an answer I'm not even sure of myself.

"Why finance?" I mutter, leaning back and rubbing my jaw. Numbers make sense to me. They always have. There's a comfort in knowing that two plus two will always be four, and that if there's a problem with numbers, it can be solved. I enjoy being the one to solve those problems.

I type out a few lines about wanting to broaden my skills and contribute more meaningfully to the business world, though the words feel stilted. At the end, I find myself adding a more honest thought: *I'm ready to try something new, to take a step forward that I've put off for too long.*

Fuck, this one-handed bullshit is so frustrating. It takes me nearly thirty minutes to fill everything out, when it should've taken me half that.

With one last look over the application, I click submit. A confirmation email appears in my inbox almost immediately, congratulating me on the first step toward my new future. It's a small thing, just an email, but seeing it there feels oddly satisfying.

CHAPTER FIVE
MARIE

My heart thumps in my chest as I set an empty notebook and a cup of pens and pencils out on an empty table near the library's front desk. Is this too much? Am I being too fussy? I don't want Garrett to think I'm being over the top, but I want to make sure he has everything he needs to work on his class assignments. Haven had called two weeks ago and asked if I'd help Garrett with his classwork once he was accepted and enrolled into the program. Of course, I immediately said yes. The chance to spend one-on-one time with the man of my dreams? Sign me the hell up!

Still, I don't want to freak him out. I try to be cool, calm, and collected around him. To be flirty and fun, but inside, I'm always a nervous mess, wanting to impress him and show him I'm an interesting, attractive woman he should pay attention to.

"Geez, are you going to serve him milk and cookies too?" Ally teases, coming up behind me and looking over my shoulder. She has open campus on Tuesdays and Thursdays, and has been coming to the library during that time to get extra SAT prep work in.

"I just want to make sure he has everything he needs," I say, defending myself as I move the pens over a little.

"Riiiight." Ally moves around me and leans against the desk so she can look me in the eye. "It's not at all because you have the biggest crush on Garrett in the history of the world. You're worse than the pick-me girls in my class."

I roll my eyes. "So I like him, so what? Wanting him to succeed isn't a crime, and neither is making sure he has everything he needs."

Laughing, Ally shakes her head and grins up at me. "You've been trying to nail down Garrett for years. Do you really think helping him study for his English class will be what convinces him to throw you a bone—literally?"

I hate how easily she sees through me. She and Haven are the only people who know the extent of my feelings for Garrett... everyone else just likes to laugh at my little "crush." Still, I'm not about to admit to the hope burning in me that this could actually be an opportunity for something more between me and Garrett.

"Ally!" I exclaim, feigning shock and pressing my hand to my chest dramatically, playing it up to hide my real anxiety. "How crude! My intentions for Garrett are pure, and I have no desire to climb him like an oak tree. For shame!"

"You're so dumb," she giggles.

"And you're in my way." I playfully shove her away from the desk.

"Man, I hope I never go as gaga over a guy as you," Ally groans. "This is sad."

"Don't you have studying you should be doing?"

She shrugs. "Yeah, but this is way more entertaining."

"Back to work," I order, pointing toward the computer station across from the one I'm setting up for Garrett. Ally's books and study materials are spread out on the desk around the monitor. "Go on, before I make you scrub down the fairy tale house in the children's section."

Ally scrunches up her nose in disgust. "Ew, gross. No, thank you. I'd rather study."

She moves back to her chair, plops down, slips her earbuds in her ears, and turns her attention to one of the SAT study books opened in front of her. I make my way back to the front reception counter, where Kathy is helping a couple of patrons check out their books. Sitting in one of the roller chairs, I focus on work for a while and try to distract myself so I don't keep glancing at the front door for Garrett.

It's about twenty minutes later when a deep, familiar voice says, "Hey, Marie. I'm here."

Startled, I look up and meet Garrett's green gaze. He's standing on the other side of the reception counter, smiling at me, a messenger bag slung over his good shoulder. His dark brown hair is a little longer than he would usually wear it, and his scruff thicker, but it gives him this rugged appearance that makes my stomach flip with instant desire. Swallowing, I give him a friendly smile and make my way over to him.

"Hey! It's good to see you on your feet. Feeling better?"

He shrugs and glances down at his arm, which is out of his cast and in a stabilizing sling.

"Mostly," he answers. "Gotta wear this thing for a bit yet. Still have some achiness, but nothing major. Feeling pretty good overall."

"That's good to hear." I push to my feet and hurry around the counter to reach him. Wrapping my hands around his good arm, I press myself against him. "Right this way. There's a place set up just for you."

He lets me steer him toward the table I've prepared for him. Ally looks up as we approach and gives Garrett a chin jerk in greeting before dropping her gaze back to her book. Letting go of Garrett's arm, I pull out the desk chair for him.

"Get comfortable," I tell him. "We need to get started."

He arches a brow at me. "Thanks, Marie, but you don't really have to help me that much. I don't want to take you away from work."

"Don't worry," I reply. "I'm happy to help, and I'll just kind of be around when you need me, okay? Let's be real. With your arm like that, you won't be able to type or write properly. So, come on. Show me your syllabus. I want to get a better idea of what you need to get done for this English class."

He sighs, but then shrugs his bag off his shoulder and hands it to me. I pull out his laptop and turn it on, and then he directs me to his school's website and we log-in to his student portal. The syllabus is a PDF, so I download it and we go over the assignments listed. Since he's in an English class, there are a lot of essays he'll have to write, and a few research papers.

"All right, so I know you can't look at a screen like this for too long," I say, "and typing with one hand will be slow, but you can stay here as long as you need. Ally and I will both be around to help you when you need us. Just don't push yourself too hard, okay?"

I stop, realizing I've been blabbering nonstop for a while, and I glance at him. Garrett is watching me with an amused grin.

"What?" I ask, frowning. "Why are you looking at me like that?"

He chuckles. "It's nothing. You're just taking charge so naturally."

My cheeks flush. "Oh, crap. I've totally taken over, haven't I? Sometimes I just get carried away. I'm sorry."

"No need to apologize," he tells me. "You're cute when you're like this."

"You... you think I'm cute?"

"Of course you're cute." He leans back in his chair and tilts his head as he looks at me. "A bit of a control freak, but I'm used to Haven bossing me around, so hanging with you will be a breeze."

I stare at him, totally taken aback. Is he flirting with me? He's never reciprocated my flirting before. We stare at each other for several long moments, and something crosses his face, softening his expression. His eyes suddenly dip. Is he looking at my lips? I instinctively lick them and his gaze narrows slightly. My heart is racing and I can't help wondering what would happen if I were just to lean in closer and...

"Marie?"

Startled, I jerk back at the sound of someone calling my name. Who the hell...?

"Marie!"

Oh, shit. It's my stepmother, Meredith. I'd recognize that grating, entitled tone anywhere. I can only imagine what she's doing here, but she's just going to keep causing a disruption in the library if I don't hurry to see what she wants. Sighing, I stand and give Garrett an apologetic look.

"Sorry, I'll be right back," I tell him before slipping past him and hurrying toward the front of the library.

I spin around and find Meredith is standing by the front desk, her brown eyes narrowed with impatience as she gazes around. She's dressed in a green wrap dress and high heels, her honey blonde hair pulled back into an elegant knot at the back of her head, and her face is smoothed out with just a little too much makeup. She's tapping her foot on the floor, clearly annoyed. I glance down and see that she's holding the hand of one of my youngest siblings, Stevie. The four-year-old has the same honey-colored hair as his mom, but my dad's dark green eyes. When he sees me, his face lights up with a wide smile.

"Marie!" he exclaims.

"Hey, little man," I say with a grin as I come to a stop in front of them. Looking up at Meredith, I give her a frustrated frown. "Meredith, you can't shout like that in the library. You're bothering everyone."

She rolls her eyes and huffs. "Don't speak to me in that condescending tone. I need you to look after Stevie for the afternoon. Your father's at work, the other kids are all in school, and I have to get to a hair appointment downtown."

I just manage to bite back an angry groan. Meredith does crap like this all the time... of course, what else is new? It doesn't matter to her if I have a job or plans or simply want to be by myself—if she needs someone to watch the kids, she expects me to do it, no matter what. It's aggravating and disrespectful, but no matter how badly I want to tell her no, I can't stand the thought of leaving my siblings in the lurch.

Stevie looks at me with such excitement, I don't want to disappoint him. I'll say yes for him, but this just shows how little regard Meredith has for me, my time, and my career.

"Meredith, I..."

"Oh, I thought that was you, Mrs. Green. You look lovely today."

Garrett is suddenly at my side, a charming smile in place as he gazes at my stepmother.

Meredith blinks and then her cheeks turn bright pink. She smiles and giggles like a teenage girl.

"Oh, Garrett, I almost didn't recognize you sitting there," she declares. "I'd heard about your accident, but you look like you're on your way to a full recovery. I'm so glad!"

"Thank you, Mrs. Green." Garrett shoots me a look and a grin before giving her his attention again. "I'm really lucky, especially since Marie agreed to help me with my schoolwork. I decided to finish my degree."

Meredith's eyes widen and her lips part.

"How wonderful!" she exclaims, looking between Garrett and me. "That's such a fantastic goal to work toward, Garrett. Well, I won't interrupt you two. I'll just have Ally look after Stevie. She's got open campus this afternoon, right? Where is Ally?"

"I'm right here, Mom," Ally groans, popping her head out from a nearby row of shelves.

Meredith gives Garrett another smile as she hurries past us to take Stevie to Ally. I stare after her, totally floored by her sudden change of demeanor. Looking back up at Garrett, I catch him staring after Meredith as well. There's a look on his face that I can't explain, but it makes me pause. Is he angry?

Before I can fully process the look, he gazes back down at me and his expression shifts in an instant. He smiles and his eyes flood with warmth, banishing any concerns from my mind.

I give him a grin.

"Thanks for that," I say.

"No problem," he replies with a wink. "Can we get back to work? I don't want to take up more of your time than necessary."

I nod, warmth flooding through me even as my concern for his wellbeing spikes. "Yep, definitely!"

He turns and starts back toward the table and I follow, watching him closely and feeling absolutely giddy.

CHAPTER SIX
GARRETT

She smells like vanilla today. Marie smells different most every day, and I've become a little obsessed with trying to figure out what each new scent is. She must have an entire collection of body sprays. I like this one a lot—truth be told; I like every scent she wears, but this one makes me think of something sweet and tasty. Something I could lick as a tasty little treat.

"Garrett? Hello? You in there?"

Blinking, I realize with a start that I've been staring at Marie without saying a word. She's watching me with a small, concerned frown.

"Oh, sorry," I murmur, clearing my throat. "Spaced out there for a bit."

"Are you okay?" she asks, looking me over and gently touching my good arm. "You're not too tired, are you? Do you have a headache? It's been nearly an hour. We can take a break if you want."

"I'm fine," I assure her. "Really, just got lost in my thoughts for a bit."

"Are you sure?"

I give her a grin. "It's been two weeks since we started this.

My headaches are few and far between and my arm is feeling tons better. I promise you, I'm totally fine."

This time I've spent with her has been both productive and confusing. She's been a tremendous help with editing my papers and working with me on the English assignments I struggle with. She's been patient, kind, and generous, giving me space to work on my own but being close by in case I need her. At some point, visiting the library became a highlight of my days. Walking in and seeing her smile... watching the way she interacts with anyone else who walks into the building... seeing the way she lights up when she talks about books... it makes me want to spend more and more time with her.

It's a slippery slope that's been difficult to avoid.

She arches a brow and gives me a skeptical look before sighing and saying, "All right, if you say so. I swear to God, if you're just trying to make me feel better, I'm going to kill you."

That makes me chuckle. Marie has always made me laugh... even when she was a mostly annoying little kid, she could come up with jokes that I thought were hilarious. No other woman has really made me laugh like she does, now that I think about it.

It's making things... complicated.

Being so close to her during our study sessions has been an unexpected torture. She's been helping me take notes and work on papers as my arm has continued to heal. I've noticed different things about her that have made it difficult to focus on my schoolwork.

Apart from her scent, there are her kissable pink lips. She parts them when she's really concentrating, and sometimes she'll press the end of her pen against her plump bottom lip. When she does that, I get the urge to pull the pen away and take her lip between my teeth.

Wait, where did that thought come from? What the hell is

wrong with me? I shouldn't be having these thoughts about Marie, but every time she brushes up against me, throws me a flirtatious smile, or walks away with her hips swaying, my cock twitches and my blood heats. Then the guilt sets in. I shouldn't be thinking of her like that. She's too young for me. She's like a sister.

Even as I tell myself that over and over again, I can't stop sneaking looks at her or imagining how her lips would feel wrapped around my cock.

She checks her phone and lets out a sigh. "Shoot, we need to finish up for the day. I need to get back to work."

"No problem," I reply, a little relieved. My thoughts are getting a little out of control, so some distance is probably for the best. "Thanks for your help."

She stands from her chair and I follow suit, but my elbow hits a textbook sitting on the edge of the desk. It falls to the floor with a clatter.

"Oh, shit," I mumble, bending down to get it.

"I'll get it," Marie says at the same time.

Our hands meet as we both touch the book and I look up, meeting her gaze. We're close. Really close. I could lean in and press my lips to hers with ease. The urge to kiss her strikes me like a lightning bolt and I wonder if it would be such a bad thing to do. Her cheeks grow rosy, and her eyes drop to my mouth. She'd let me kiss her if I tried. She wants me to. I can see it in her heated gaze...

"Are you two all right?"

I jump, startled at the sudden intrusion, and look up to find Kathy standing over us. She's watching us with a furrowed brow and a concerned frown. Embarrassment floods through me, as if I've been caught doing something I shouldn't be doing. Clearing my throat, I grab the book and stand back up. Not looking at Marie, I quickly gather my things.

"I'll see you later," I say, flashing her a smile before turning to hurry away, leaving Marie and the temptation she presents behind me.

LATER THAT NIGHT, I'm still thinking about Marie, despite my best efforts to put her out of my head. She's somehow burrowed her way into my thoughts and won't let go. Sitting on my couch, I dangle a half-empty beer bottle between my fingers and rest my head back to stare up at the ceiling. I run my free hand over my face and let out a long, frustrated breath. I keep picturing that moment when our hands met and her lips were right there, begging to be kissed. What if I'd done it? What would have happened? That's a dangerous road for me to go down, but I can't stop imagining her spread out on the library floor beneath me, her cheeks flushed and her lips plump and reddened from my kiss.

Fuck... I need to get it together. I need to remember why I can't cross that line with her.

As much as I hate to remember it, I force myself to think back to one of the last conversations I had with my mom, not long before she died.

She'd been in the hospital, sickly and gaunt. Weak. Fading. I hated seeing her like that, and I hate even more that I didn't visit her as often as I should have because the sight of her in so much pain gutted me.

I'd made myself go that day. I'm still not sure why, but some instinct pulled at me to go to her. Maybe a part of me knew she had little time left. That if I didn't see her then, I might never get the chance to again.

She'd smiled, putting on a brave face for me, but I could tell she was suffering. We both knew it was almost the end, but I refused to say so out loud.

Mom was braver than me.

She took my hand in hers. Her skin was paper thin and her bones felt brittle wrapped in mine.

Meeting my gaze, she spoke in a low, raspy voice.

"Gary, I need you to promise me something."

"Anything, Mom."

"Take care of yourself when I'm gone, and look after my girls. Both of them. They're going to need you."

With tears in my eyes, I nodded and said, *"I promise. I'll take care of them."*

Her girls—Haven and Marie.

Marie was like a second daughter to my mom. Her mother had been best friends with mine, and when she'd died, mom had unofficially "adopted" Marie. She loved her and cared for her, looking out for her even after her dad remarried. I remember when she'd come over as a little girl to play with Haven and how Mom doted on both girls. The two of them together were often annoying and got on my nerves, but once they were older, it wasn't so bad being around them. At some point, Marie really became part of the family. I started thinking of her as another little sister. Mom made me promise again and again to look after both her girls.

I'm glad Marie had my mom. Meredith has never really treated Marie like her daughter. Haven always complained when they were teenagers about how demanding of Marie her stepmother was, and that treatment has continued into adulthood. She treats her more like an assistant—someone she can dump her extra work and responsibilities onto and assumes Marie will take it all with a smile on her face.

It always pissed me off, and when I saw Meredith doing the same at the library the other week, I couldn't just sit back and let her take advantage of Marie. I'd had to step in and do something.

The point is, I promised my mom I'd take care of Marie, just like I would Haven. That I'd protect her and look out for her. Like a sister.

I can't break that promise to Mom. I can't have these thoughts about Marie. She's my responsibility, and I can only imagine what Mom would think if she knew I was even entertaining any kind of desire for her. She'd be disappointed, I'm sure. Disgusted, maybe... I don't know.

Leaning forward, I take a long drink of my beer. I feel an ache in my chest and can't decide if it's my heart or my ribs. They're healed, but now and then I still get a pang of discomfort. I'm doing well healing physically, but mentally, I'm a mess. Maybe having Marie help me study wasn't such a good idea after all. It's leaving me all twisted up inside and confused. The only thing that seems certain is my promise to Mom. I have to hold on to that. It was her dying wish for me, and I will not let her down.

Finishing my beer, I stand and move to set the bottle by the sink in the kitchen. Sucking in a deep breath, I steel my resolve. Marie is off limits. That's all there is to it. I'll protect her, care for her, and make sure she knows she still belongs in my family, even though mom is gone.

It can't be more than that. No matter how delicious she smells or how kissable her lips might be, I cannot cross that line with her.

CHAPTER SEVEN

MARIE

Opening the door to my house, I let out a sigh of relief. It's been a long day, and I'm exhausted. I think having Garrett in the library for the last few weeks has gone well... I haven't acted too awkward. I hope.

All I want to do right now is sit down with a glass of wine, put my feet up, and relax.

Dumping my purse next to the door and kicking off my shoes, I shuffle down the hall and into my kitchen. My house is small and outdated, but it's cozy and the appliances in the galley kitchen are all shiny and new. When I moved in, I painted the wood cabinets white to make the space appear a little lighter and more open, and the tile floor and laminate countertops are all clean and in decent shape. I grab an unopened bottle of wine from the little rack on top of my fridge and set it on the counter. Humming to myself, I pull out a glass and the bottle opener, but just as I'm about to pop the cork free, my phone buzzes.

Pulling my phone from my pocket, I roll my eyes. *Step-Monster* flashes across the screen. Meredith. No, thank you...

However, as I set the phone on the counter, ready to ignore it, guilt immediately slams through me. Shit... what if something's really wrong? With a frustrated groan, I pick the phone back up and answer the call.

"Hey, Meredith. What's up?"

"Marie, the little ones got home from school today sick with the flu," she says without preamble. "We need you to let Ally stay over there until the kids are better. She has so much happening at school, plus her SAT test is coming up. Your father and I don't want her to get sick too, so she has to stay with you."

It's not a question or a request, but it never is. This is the fourth time just this week she and Dad have had me take care of the kids—one morning, I had to drop the twins off at school, then I had to keep the youngest with me in the library, pick up groceries, and on and on.

"Meredith, I..."

"Your dad is on his way over to drop Ally off," Meredith says, as if I wasn't speaking at all.

"What?" I gasp. "But how did you even know I'd be home? What if I had plans?"

"Do you?"

I hesitate, "Well... no."

"Then there's no problem."

That's not the point, but of course, Meredith doesn't get that, or she just doesn't care. Still, I think of Ally. I want her to be successful and go to a good college, and I'll help her however I can. None of this is her fault, so... I'll suck it up for my sister's sake.

"All right," I murmur. "She can stay here."

"We'll let you know when the little ones are feeling better," Meredith says. "Make sure Ally does her homework. She can't fall behind."

"Got it."

Meredith hangs up without so much as a goodbye or a thank you.

I set my phone down and finish opening the bottle of wine, pouring myself a big glass. Meredith is such a... no. No, I can't think that. She's my father's wife and the mother of my siblings. Even if she doesn't give a shit about me or respect me, I need to respect her—for them.

Even if she is a narcissistic bitch.

Meredith has never liked me. At first, she tried to be nice for my dad's sake, but she's not the type of woman who likes to come in second place. That she's Dad's second wife has always been a thorn in her side, even if she won't admit it out loud. She'd rather forget that my mom ever existed, but I'm a constant and unavoidable reminder that Meredith wasn't my dad's first love. I don't know how someone can be jealous of a dead woman, but Meredith is.

Irritated, I take a long drink. The wine is fruity and warm as it slides down my throat and into my belly. It's nice, and it helps me relax a bit.

I take another drink just as my doorbell rings. That's probably Dad and Ally. Setting my glass down, I trudge to the front door and open it, forcing a smile.

My dad is a tall man, and he used to be bulkier, but he's lost weight over the years and is long and lean now. He has graying brown hair and those dark green eyes that haven't held the same warmth for me since my mom died. He's looking at me now with the flat, cool expression he seems to reserve only for me. Ally stands next to him, her hazel eyes—just like Meredith's— wide and apologetic as she gazes up at me. She's got her backpack slung over one shoulder and is also holding onto a small duffle bag.

"Meredith called?" Dad asks.

"Yep, she did."

"Good. Hopefully, it's only for a few days, but we don't want to risk Ally getting sick."

"Dad, I'm fine..." Ally protests.

He shakes his head and tells her, "Sweetie, you've got too much happening right now. This is an important time for you, and your mom and me want to make sure nothing gets in your way."

Watching them, I see the father I knew when I was younger. Warm, concerned, caring. He's like that with all his children with Meredith, which is good. With me, though... I'm not sure what I ever did to lose his affection. I think it's mostly because I look so much like Mom and he can't handle that, but I know Meredith has influenced his attitude toward me. He was always eager to please her when they first got together, and she's been so critical of me that her opinions slowly bled into his own. I think he got tired of the strain I apparently put on their marriage, though I never did anything significant to cause that. Between the kids and the pressure from Meredith, at some point he just decided it was easier to keep me at arm's length. I don't have the heart to tell him how much that bothers me.

I keep my expression neutral as he turns back to me, careful not to let him see the hurt I'm feeling.

"We need you to run some errands for us as well," he says, his expression going cool again as he glances at my wine glass. "I'm going to text you a list of things we need from the grocery store and drugstore for the kids. We'll be fine for tonight, since you've decided to start drinking already, but we'll need every-thing picked up and dropped off in the morning. Meredith is going to stay home from work, but I have to be in the office early."

I clench my hands into fists, digging my fingernails into my palms.

"Dad, I have work too..."

He scoffs. "I'm sure the library can handle itself without you for an hour or two. The books aren't going anywhere, and your family needs your help, Marie. Get your priorities straight."

I bristle at the dismissive tone he uses to discuss my job. He's never taken my career seriously and even has called me a glorified babysitter since I work with a lot of the children's programming at the library. The disrespect isn't anything new, but it always pisses me off.

"I can't leave Kathy in the lurch like that," I snap. "That's not fair to her."

Dad rolls his eyes. "I doubt you'll be busy in the morning, anyway. School is in session. Who shows up at the library anymore?"

This conversation is going nowhere. I know that nothing I say will convince him that my job is legitimate and important. It's like a punch to the gut, every single time.

I open my mouth to argue further, but he waves his hand dismissively.

"I need to go," he declares. "Ally, be good, study hard, and call if you need anything."

He plants a kiss on her forehead and turns to leave, giving me a half-hearted wave. I watch him reach his car, climb inside, and drive off.

There are so many things I wish I could say to my father. I wish I could find the courage to tell him just how much he hurts me. To demand to know when and why he apparently stopped loving me, but that's what it feels like most of the time. I'm just a thing in his life that he has to put up with. A reminder of the life and family he had before his current one. Sometimes I think that, if he could, he'd cut me off and pretend like there was nothing before Meredith and the kids. That my mom and I didn't even exist.

The only thing that keeps me from actually hating him is the knowledge that Mom's death devastated him. He wasn't the same after we lost her, and I know his treatment of me comes from a place of deep, unending pain. That obviously doesn't make it fair to me, but I can at least understand the source of his coldness toward me.

"You okay?" Ally asks me, touching my hand, pulling my attention to her.

I force a smile for her sake and nod. "Yeah, I'm fine. Dad just being Dad. Come on in. I need to get the guest room ready, but let's sit and chill for a bit."

Her expression is sympathetic, but I push down my pain and step aside to let her into the house. We make our way to the living room and Ally drops her bags on the floor before we settle together on the couch. Ally tilts her head and studies me with a slightly furrowed brow.

"I'm sorry," she says. "I tried to convince them that I didn't need to come here and that we shouldn't bother you, but they wouldn't listen."

"It's not your fault." I assure her. "Don't worry. You know I love having you here."

"Still, it's not fair," she insists. "Mom and Dad can be so selfish sometimes."

As much as I appreciate Ally's understanding and that she tries to stand up for me, I don't want her to resent Meredith and Dad because of me.

I lean back against the couch, deciding it's best to steer the conversation away from our parents and into safer territory.

"Tell me about school. And not about your studies or the SATs. Tell me about fun stuff."

Ally's face lights up and her lips curl into a big grin.

"Okay!" she exclaims, and I think she might be relieved to

focus on something other than her grades, tests, and college prospects. "So, you remember my friend Rebecca? Well, the other day, she…"

I sit back and listen as Ally rattles on, warmth flooding me at her enthusiasm and excitement—as if she's just been waiting for the opportunity to talk about this stuff. She tells me about her favorite teacher, her plans to audition for the school play, and even a prank war going on in her science class that I make her promise she won't participate in. Then she tilts her head, giving me a curious look.

"So… what's going on with you and Garrett?"

I blink, surprised by the sudden change in topic.

"Garrett? Nothing more than usual. Why?"

She shrugs, grinning. "You've been spending so much time together, I was just curious if you'd made any progress on that front."

I laugh. "I wish I could say I have, but no. I'm just like a sister to him, and I don't think that's changing now that I'm helping him while he's hurt."

Ally giggles, then looks thoughtful. "What was it like growing up around him and Haven?"

Another question I hadn't anticipated. Ally's being oddly insightful tonight—not that she isn't usually. She's such a smart girl. Observant, witty, and caring. She's easy to talk to, and we have fun together despite our age difference.

As I consider her question, my thoughts drift back to when I was a girl. How I'd go to Haven's house almost every day because her mom reminded me of my mom so much - they were best friends, after all, so shared a lot of similar qualities - and I was little and just wanted that love and attention so badly. Their mom had embraced me like I was her own daughter and she made me feel like I belonged with them.

"We were all really close," I tell her, trying to keep my tone casual. "Haven's practically my sister, and her family just... became part of mine too, you know? Then there was Garrett. He was always protective of us. Always looking out for us when he was in high school. Even though he was ten years older and had a whole life of his own, he was always there for Haven and me, even when he went off to college. He didn't have to be there for me, but he was. He always made me feel... precious."

Ally's quiet, watching me with a funny little smile, and she raises an eyebrow. "So, you're in love with him."

I roll my eyes. Of course, I'm in love with Garrett. I have been since I was eighteen. I've always tried to hide the depth of my feelings for him by keeping things light and flirty.

"Keep that up," I tease, "and I'll send you right back to the flu den, where you belong."

She laughs, stretching her arms over her head. "I can handle a cold, thank you very much."

My brow furrows in confusion. "Wait, what do you mean, a cold?"

Ally shrugs. "The twins just have colds. It's really not that big a deal. I don't know why Mom and Dad are freaking out so much. They probably picked it up when we went to the water park for their birthday this past weekend, not the school."

My stomach clenches. Birthday party? I'd asked if they were doing anything for the twins, and Meredith had told me they were too busy and might plan something later this month. She lied. She fucking lied to me to keep me away. Why am I even surprised? It's not the first time this kind of thing has happened, and no doubt she made up some excuse to justify my absence or make me the bad guy somehow.

I'm only part of this family when it's convenient for Meredith and Dad... otherwise, I might as well not exist.

For Ally's sake, I hide my anger and frustration because this isn't her fault, but deep down, I'm fuming, hurt, and disappointed.

But most of all, I'm tired. Tired of being disappointed—and tired of having no real place in my own family.

CHAPTER EIGHT
GARRETT

Something's up. Marie is being way too quiet today. She hasn't even tried flirting with me since I arrived at the library, which is really not like her. I glance from my computer screen over to her and frown, concern making my stomach twist. She's just sitting in her chair, staring down at an open notebook where she's been reading over the notes I've taken for the paper I'm working on. The library is pretty much empty right now, which should be a good thing because that means I have more of her attention, but somehow it doesn't feel that way today.

"Hey," I say gently. "Are you okay?"

Marie looks up, blinking, and appears momentarily startled.

"Huh? Oh, sorry, I spaced out. I'm okay. Are you okay? Do you have a headache?"

I don't believe her. I've always been able to tell when she's not being truthful, and the frustration in her gaze, even as she tries to hide it, is a dead giveaway. It causes a heavy feeling to settle in my chest. I want her to be her usual bubbly, funny self.

"No, no headache. Come on," I say, turning in my chair so I can face her fully. "I know there's something going on. Tell me. Maybe I can help."

Whatever is bothering her, I have the overwhelming urge to fix it for her.

She lets out a long sigh and shakes her head. "I doubt it. It's not really something that can be fixed, I don't think."

"Still, tell me," I insist. "I want to know."

She stares at me before finally saying, "It's Meredith... shocking, I know. She did the most unbelievable thing last night and told me my youngest siblings were sick with the flu and that Ally needed to come stay with me. Mind you, I don't mind having Ally over, but it wasn't a question or a request—Meredith simply declared that Ally was staying with me and I didn't have a say in the matter. Then, it turns out the kids don't even have the flu! They just have colds that they got from their birthday party this last weekend, which I wasn't invited to! Meredith totally lied to me, but that really shouldn't surprise me. She's never had any qualms about lying to my face to get what she wants. This isn't even the worst one, but it's just so... ugh! I can't stand her most of the time."

She stops talking abruptly and stares at me with wide eyes, panting. I'm a bit stunned by her rant and don't immediately know what to say.

"Oh, my gosh," she quickly says, her cheeks turning bright pink. "I'm sorry. I didn't mean to go off like that."

"Don't apologize," I tell her. "You can vent to me about this stuff."

"Thanks," she murmurs, her shoulders slumping as she drops her head in her hands. "This is so embarrassing."

Embarrassing? She thinks expressing her genuine feelings about how unfair her stepmother treats her is embarrassing? She should be as furious as I am hearing how Meredith manipulates her so badly. It's not right. Marie is one of the most selfless people I know. She'd do just about anything for the people she cares about, and that her stepmother would take advantage of that is infuriating.

"You should start telling Meredith no. Stand up for yourself against her. She can't keep treating you this way."

Whatever response I might have expected from her, it's not her frowning up at me with narrowed eyes.

"I want to be there for my siblings," she insists defensively. "I need to be able to help them. Yeah, Meredith's a pain in the ass, but I'm not doing any of this for her. I'm doing it for them."

"I get that, Marie," I reply, firmly. "But you can be there for your siblings without letting Meredith or your dad walk all over you. You have a right to set boundaries."

She scoffs. "You're one to talk about boundaries. Aren't you always dropping everything to help everyone else instead of pursuing your own dreams and plans?"

Her words are sharp and feel like a slap in the face. Anger pulses through me and I glare back at her.

"At least my family is appreciative of what I do for them. I'm not just running around helping people who don't give a damn about me otherwise."

She sucks in a sharp breath and pushes to her feet, sending her chair scratching along the floor.

"God, you're such an asshole sometimes!" she exclaims in a hushed tone, ever the librarian. "Why do I waste my time with you?"

Attempting to stand as well, I get immediately dizzy, so sit back down, and look up at her. I'm so fucking over these lingering concussion symptoms. I snap, "I don't know, maybe because you're stubborn and don't know what's good for you."

She lets out a huff of irritation and turns, apparently intent on storming away from me. I'm not done with her, though. Now I stand and I grab her hand with my good arm and spin her back around, yanking her into my chest. I wince when my shoulder is jostled, but ignore the pain as I hold her against me. She gasps, her hands falling flat against my pecs, and she gives me a venomous look.

"What do you think you're doing, you brut?"

My lips crashing against hers cut off her furious tirade. I can't help myself. She's pressed up tight against me, looking gorgeous in her fury, and my blood is so heated with anger and arousal, I can't control myself.

She moans against my mouth and parts her lips, letting my tongue tangle with hers. Her hands slide up my chest and grip my shoulders, and I grab hold of her hips. As I move my lips over hers, I lose myself in the feel of her. Her soft body pressed tight against mine feels so damn right. I love the sound of her soft breaths and whimpers as I explore her mouth and run my hands up her back, slipping them beneath her shirt to touch her bare skin.

Fuck, she's so soft. So lush. I could get addicted to the taste of her. She returns my kiss eagerly, clinging to me so sweetly that I can't stop my imagination from running wild, and now I'm picturing her on her knees, gazing up at me with those big eyes and this sweet mouth parted and ready for what I have to give her.

"Garrett," she suddenly murmurs, her tone low and needy.

The sound of my name—the one only she calls me—snaps me back to reality. Damn it... what am I doing? I can't be like this with her. I can't cross this line.

"*...take care of my girls...*"

Mom's voice rings through my head and guilt slams through me. I break the kiss and quickly step away from her, pulling myself out of her arms. I'm dizzy and my head is throbbing, but it's not just my concussion punishing me. It's my shame as well. She looks startled and frowns up at me, confusion mixing in with the lingering heat in her eyes.

"Garrett... what?" She's panting, looking beautiful all flustered.

"Sorry, I have to go," I mumble, turning and grabbing my stuff, thankful no one was around to see what had just happened. "I'll see you later."

She stares after me, her jaw dropped, as I hurry away from her.

***

FUCKING DAMN IT! Why did I do that? Why did I kiss her?

Laying in bed later that night, I stare up at my ceiling, unable to sleep as I replay my kiss with Marie repeatedly. It was such a mistake, and now that I've had a taste of her, my body is demanding more. Even now, my cock is rock hard as I remember the feel of her curves in my hands and her tongue sweeping across my lips.

What would have happened if we hadn't stopped? If I hadn't pulled away, I'm not sure I would've been able to stop myself. My mind latches onto this thought and runs with it. I imagine that I'm kissing her still, but instead of breaking from her and running away, I turn her around and press her against the desk. She moans and tilts her head back, and I run my lips down her throat. I slide my hands up the front of her shirt and cup her breasts.

"We shouldn't do this here," she whimpers, but she doesn't sound like she objects to this at all.

"I can't wait," I growl, and in my head, we're totally alone. There's no one else anywhere in the library, and I'm no longer confined in a sling. *"Nobody else is here. I want you. Now."*

Shit, I can't resist. I shove my good hand into my boxer shorts and grip my cock. As my fantasy continues to play out in my head, I stroke my shaft hard and fast.

"Let me make you feel good," she purrs, slipping off the desk and lowering herself to her knees in front of me.

Holding my gaze, she unzips my pants and pulls my cock free. With a sultry grin, she licks me from base to tip. Pleasure shoots through me like lightning. I arch my hips off my bed, wishing she was really here, wrapping those plump lips around the head of my cock and sliding down, taking me deep into her mouth.

"You're so sexy," I hiss. *"This feels so good."*

She hums around me, and I shudder, squeezing my shaft tighter, matching my strokes to the rhythm of her head, imagining her bobbing up and down, sucking me so perfectly. I want more. I want her. This fantasy isn't enough. Grabbing her head, I start thrusting and she takes me with no trouble. It's good... so, so good. My orgasm builds within me. It twists into a tight ball deep inside my belly.

"Marie," I groan out loud, keeping my eyes squeezed shut so I don't lose the image of her sucking me. "Fuck... Marie!"

"You've wanted this for such a long time, haven't you?"

I have—God, I want her.

"You know I want you too, Garrett. You don't need to resist me anymore."

I won't. I won't resist you. I can't, Marie... you're everything I've ever wanted.

"I want you to come for me, Garrett Please."

Yes. Yes, yes, yes. I want that. Open your mouth, Marie. Take me, baby. This is all for you.

She flashes me an eager smile and the hunger in her eyes is just what I need to push me over the edge.

Throwing my head back, I let out a long, guttural groan as my orgasm slams through me. My body jerks and spasms and it just goes on and on. When the waves have passed and I'm left breathless, barely satisfied and back in reality, the guilt rushes back in. Stabbing my hands into my hair, I moan in frustration and anger at myself.

I'm such a son of a bitch.

I need to get a hold of myself. Disgust rolls through me for giving into my baser desires when I'm usually in more control than this.

Dropping my hands, I ball my fists into my sheets and take several long breaths to slow my racing heart. That's enough. I have to bring this to an end. The kiss with Marie was a mistake, and one I will not repeat. Nothing more will happen than that. I refuse to break my promise to my mother.

I can't deny that I want Marie. That I'm attracted to her. Fine. I acknowledge those feelings and desires. That doesn't mean they get to control me.

After today, I will not touch Marie again, and no matter how difficult it might be, I'm going to push these inappropriate thoughts of her out of my head.

CHAPTER NINE
MARIE

I stare up at my bedroom ceiling, completely exhausted after a night tossing and turning. Groaning, I press the palms of my hands against my eyes. A headache builds in my temples. It's going to be a rough day, and it's all Garrett's fault. Him and his heart-stopping kiss. I haven't been able to get it out of my head. The little sleep I got was overwhelmed with dreams about Garrett and that damn kiss, but also of him running away right after.

Fuck, that was humiliating. He was the one who kissed me first! What gave him the right to flee like I was trying to jump him in the middle of the library? Talk about mixed signals. I'm more confused about his feelings for me than ever. Maybe if I had better insight into how his mind works... only one person who knows Garrett better than me.

Rolling over, I grab my cell phone off my side-table and shoot a text to Haven.

Marie: Hey! Are you free today after work?

Haven: Sure am!

Marie: Do you want to meet up? Brew Ridge?

Haven: Sounds good.

Thank God. Haven will give me some advice for handling Garrett. To understand exactly what happened yesterday.

Why did he run away? I thought the kiss was great—intense and arousing. When his lips touched mine, it felt like a fire blazed to life deep in my belly. The kiss felt so right, so perfect, better than I had ever imagined. I hadn't wanted it to end. I'd thought that, at last, he was seeing me as the woman I am and not the little girl he seemed to hold on to his mind.

But, apparently, I'd been wrong.

Throwing my blanket aside, I climb out of bed and shuffle into my bathroom to get ready for the day. Ally has already left for school for the day. I try not to think of Garrett, but I can't erase the image of him running away out of my mind, no matter how hard I try. It's going to be so awkward seeing him today… if he even shows up. Maybe he'll decide he doesn't want my help anymore after all. I mean, it's not like it's essential that I help him. He's got a week until his next paper is due—it would be slow going with one hand, but he could write it all by himself. I don't know how to approach this situation.

I head into work with a knot in my stomach. It's going to be okay. We're both adults. We can talk about this. Handle the fallout of that kiss and him running away with all the maturity and grace of a teenage boy. Yeah… yeah, that's what we'll do. It'll be fine. No problem at all.

Walking into the library, I'm afraid my heart is going to burst because it's racing so fast. I make my way to the reception desk, give Kathy a quick hello, and plop down behind my computer. Determined not to worry about Garrett, I do my best to focus on work for the morning. Garrett shows up early in the afternoons to do his schoolwork, but about noon, I get a text from him.

> Garrett: Hey, sorry, I can't make it today. I'll see you tomorrow, maybe.

Oh... shit.

Slumping back in my chair, I release a long breath of disappointment. Things are now so awkward, he doesn't even want to be around me anymore. I can read right through that 'maybe'... I don't think he's going to come back to the library.

I make it through the rest of the workday despite my glum mood, doing my best not to let it show around Kathy or the kids who come in for story time after school. When I get done, I collect my stuff, say goodbye to Kathy, and head to the coffee shop to meet Haven.

She's already there when I arrive, sitting at a table in the corner, two drinks in front of her. When she sees me, she smiles and waves. I hurry over to her.

"Hey!" I say, reaching the table. "Thanks for meeting me."

"No problem, girlie." She pushes a cup toward me. "I got you your latte."

"You're an angel," I sigh, sliding into the seat across from her. "What are you drinking?"

"Tea." She holds up her cup and takes a sip. "God, I miss coffee."

"I can't imagine," I grumble. "I think I'd die."

Haven grins and rests a hand on her belly.

"Yeah, it'll be worth it in the end," she says.

"I have no doubt about that." I gaze at her, warmth spreading through me. She looks tired, but happy. Really, really happy.

"So," she says, looking up at me and arching a brow, "what did you want to talk about? Don't get me wrong, I love having a spontaneous girl hang out, but I get the sense that there's something else behind this coffee date."

God, she knows me so well.

I hesitate, choosing my words carefully before I decide to just yank the bandage off and get it over with.

"All right, so you know that I've been helping Garrett with his schoolwork," I say, and she nods. "Well, something happened yesterday..."

Haven's eyes go wide. "What? What happened?"

"We... we kissed."

"You did!" she exclaims so loudly that other customers turn to look at us.

My cheeks burn with embarrassment, and I try to hide my face with my hands. "Hey! Will you chill out, psycho? I don't need the whole town knowing about this."

"Okay, okay," Haven says in a much lower voice. "Sorry, but tell me more."

I give her a breakdown of what happened at the library. How Garrett and I argued and then he pulled me into that heart-stopping kiss. Of course, I also tell her how he turned tail and ran right afterward, then sent me that text with the 'maybe.' I'm positive it's just his way of blowing me off in a polite way. Haven rolls her eyes at that.

"Garrett, you moron," she grumbles.

"You can see why I'm confused and cautious. I don't think he enjoyed the kiss as much as I did, which really sucks. How am I supposed to act around him now?"

Haven shakes her head. "Marie, I love my brother. He's a wonderful man and was my rock when Mom got sick. However, that doesn't mean I can't acknowledge when he's being a total idiot. I'm sorry he left you like that, and trust me, if I thought it'd help, I'd go hunt him down and chew his ass out for doing it. We both know that's not going to change anything, though."

"What do I do?"

"I think you just need to give him some time," she answers. "Garrett's always been reserved and serious. When Dad died, he thought he needed to take on the role of man-of-the-house, even though he was still a kid. In his mind, he had to take care of me and Mom and make sure our needs were always put above his. When Mom got sick, that sense of responsibility he felt only intensified. Now I'm afraid he doesn't really know how to take care of himself. It's like he thinks if he ever dares to want something for himself, he's somehow letting everyone else down."

I consider her words and murmur, "Do you think there's really any chance for me with him, Haven? Be honest. Am I just wasting my time with him?"

"Marie, I honestly think that you and Garrett would be so good together." Haven gives me a sympathetic look and reaches across the table to take my hand. "I think your personalities complement each other and I would love to see two of my favorite people happy and settled. Garrett is... well, he's fucking stubborn. I think what you have to figure out is whether you're willing to risk him never realizing just how great you could be for him. If he were to acknowledge that and let you in, I'd put money on you two going all the way. However, if he can't get past whatever is blocking him from seeing that—seeing you—I... I don't know, Marie. I don't want you to get hurt."

It's not exactly the reassuring pep talk I was hoping for, but Haven isn't going to blow smoke up my ass just to make me feel better. That's one reason she's my best friend. I can trust her to tell me the truth.

I drum my fingers against the side of my coffee cup and consider her words.

"Part of me thinks I should just give up. I can't help but wonder if I'm pathetic for still wanting him after all these years, or just desperate. When I think about being with someone else, though, it just feels... wrong. I've wanted Garrett for so long now. No one else has ever caught my attention like he has."

"You've dated, though," Haven points out. "You've had boyfriends. So, at least you know you can be with someone else."

Chuckling sadly, I shake my head. "No, if anything, those relationships have only proven that I can't make it work with anyone else because I can't get over him."

"Why him?" Haven asks, tilting her head and studying me closely. "I know you've liked him forever, but you've never really told me why you're so obsessed with him. Why can no other man measure up to my brother?"

I rest my elbow on the table and lean into my hand, pinching the bridge of my nose.

"When Dad and Meredith got married, I was really hopeful that I'd finally have a family again," I softly explain, the memories pushing forward and warming my heart. "Dad was never the same after Mom died, and if it weren't for you and your family, I'd have been totally alone and miserable. Even after marrying Meredith, Dad didn't really change, and she obviously didn't want to be a real mother to me. You and your mom stepped in and made me feel loved and accepted... but Garrett, he made me feel safe. I looked up to him and wasn't so afraid of the world because I knew he was in it, looking out for me.

"I remember when I was dating this guy who was older and a real jerk. We'd met at *Carson's* and I really only started seeing him to try and get over Garrett. One night, I was with this guy and it was a bad date. He was being rude and pushy, and I just wanted to go home. I tried to call my dad to come get me, but he didn't pick up, so I called your house instead. Garrett answered and immediately came to get me. When my date tried to guilt me into staying out with him, Garrett got in his face and told him to back off. He defended me when my father couldn't be bothered to even answer the phone. After he chased the guy off, he took me to get ice cream and then drove around until I felt better. It was that night, I think, that I actually started to love him."

Haven gazes at me with a concerned frown. "I never knew that. You didn't tell me that story before."

I shrug. "Yeah, I know. I was embarrassed, and think I wanted that night to be between me and Garrett, something that was just ours. That sounds stupid, I know, but..."

"It's not stupid," Haven assures me, offering a reassuring hand on my shoulder. "I get it. It's kind of an anchor moment for you."

"That's a good way of putting it." Leaning back in my seat, I gaze up at the ceiling before continuing, "But maybe I've been holding onto that too tightly. Maybe I've built all this up in my head and it doesn't actually mean anything to Garrett."

"Hey, stop that," Haven orders, giving me a stern look that reminds me of how her mom would look whenever we got into trouble. "Don't give up yet. You and Garrett kissed, and he got freaked out. That doesn't mean he doesn't feel anything. If anything, I'd say that shows that he does feel something. He might not understand it yet, but if you give up, he never will."

I stare at her, surprised by her sudden vehemence. What she's saying makes sense, but I'm almost too scared to hope.

Still, knowing she believes in me and thinks there's a chance...

"I won't give up," I promise her. "Not yet."

She smiles, clearly satisfied.

"Good," she says. "You're not the type of woman who gives

up on what she wants, and I'm not going to let my brother be what breaks you of that."

I grin and chuckle, shaking my head as I pick my coffee up and take another drink. She's right. I'm not the type to give up that easily, and I won't give up hope that someday Garrett will finally see me as more than just his little sister's best friend.

CHAPTER TEN
GARRETT

The words on my computer screen blur together. Shaking my head, I try to focus on what I'm reading, but I can't make anything make sense. The open page of the notebook next to me is filled with scribbles and doodles, but nothing actually coherent.

Damn it. I can't concentrate.

It's hard to study in my apartment kitchen—being in the library just kind of set the academic mood. Helped me focus and get in the right headspace. It's been a week since I've been there. Not since my kiss with Marie. Instead, I've been working at home alone, doing my best not to give myself headaches—or, at least, attempting to. My concussion symptoms are minimal, and I'm able to go around without my sling unless I feel discomfort. Honestly, I'd rather go to the library, especially since I'm more mobile, but I've been weighed down by guilt. I'm also afraid that if I'm alone with Marie, I'll want to kiss her again.

It just felt so damn good.

Kissing her felt right. Natural. Like something we're always meant to be doing, and that freaks me the hell out.

I thought if I stayed away from her, these feelings would

disappear, but they didn't. If anything, I've only become more consumed by her.

Giving up, I sit back in my chair and run a hand over my face with a groan.

Fuck, this is such a mess. Marie has been such an incredible help to me with my classwork. I hadn't realized just how much I relied on her until I stopped doing so. Why does she have to be so incredible? So selfless? In the days since I've seen her, I've been reflecting on our history. She's always so willing to help anyone in need, including Haven and me. When Haven had issues in high school with some stupid mean girls, Marie came roaring to her defense. When Mom got sick, she'd show up to help clean the house, cook Mom food, and even sat with her a few times when she was going through chemo if I was out in the oil fields and Haven couldn't get away from work.

Marie has always been there for us... for me. Despite the fact that her own family demands her time, I know for a fact they aren't nearly as grateful to her as Haven and I are. There's just so much goodness in her. So much generosity and compassion. It only makes me more determined to protect her. Now it feels like I have to protect her from my raging lust for her.

Standing, I cross to my fridge, yank open the door, and grab a can of beer from the top shelf. Cracking it open, I take a long drink, willing the alcohol to dull the sharp feelings rolling through me. One beer is far from enough to do that, and I'm not going to let myself fall down that slippery slope of drinking to numb everything. Instead, I force myself to remember Mom and how much she loved Marie.

A memory suddenly bubbles up in my mind. Back when I was in college the first time, during my sophomore year, I went home for fall break. Haven and Marie were just kids—like nine, I'm pretty sure. Marie was at our house nearly every day that I was home, which wasn't unusual, but I'd always kind of figured as she got older, she'd be with her family more often, especially since she had younger siblings. That just wasn't the case, and I couldn't help my curiosity, so I talked to my mom about it one day.

"Is something wrong with Marie's family?" I asked. *"She's here all the time. Doesn't her dad or stepmom ever worry about her or want her home?"*

My mom and I had been standing in the kitchen and the girls had been upstairs playing in Haven's room. She gazed out the window over the sink at them and sighed.

"Things at home for Marie are... difficult," she'd told me. *"Meredith is hard on her and isn't always a great mother-figure. She likes it here, and I like having her here. When she's here, she can just have fun and be a kid. She doesn't have to worry about anything else. Plus, she reminds me of her mom, so I like having her around."*

"I remember how close you and Mrs. Green were," I murmured. *"But Marie was just seven when her mom died... how much does she remember of your friendship with Mrs. Green?"*

My mom gave me a patient look, her gaze soft and mouth curved into a gentle smile.

"She might not, but I do, and I'm not about to let her little girl grow up questioning whether or not she's truly loved. I want you to look after her, Garrett. Protect her just like you would Haven."

Back then, as a stupid college sophomore with no patience for my sister and her friend, I didn't fully understand what she meant. I have a better idea now of what she was trying to tell me, especially after the promise I made to her to take care of both girls. Marie is supposed to be like a sister to me... but it's getting harder and harder to think of her in that way.

I can't deny that I'm attracted to her. It'd be pretty stupid to even try, especially after that kiss. Guilt continues to swirl within me, but I have to figure this out.

My thoughts are interrupted by my phone ringing. I go back to the table and grab it. When I see that it's Christian, I answer.

"Hey."

"Hey, man," Christian greets. "It's time for your afternoon check-in to make sure you aren't being stupid. How's it going? How are you feeling?"

"Good," I assure him. I feel like I've been saying that a lot lately. It's my go to response to that question. I could talk about the occasional twinges my shoulder gets, or the ache in my ribs when I twist a certain way too quickly, but most people who ask me how I am don't really want those details. They want assurances that I'm good, so that's what I tell them.

Christian isn't everyone, so I know I could go into more detail with him, but I have a gut feeling that he's not actually calling me to check in on my recovery. I've been keeping him updated on how I'm doing, so there's something else he wants to talk about.

"Glad to hear it," he says.

"Is that what you're really calling about?"

Christian chuckles. "Can't get anything past you, can I?"

"Nope," I assured him with a grin. "I'm too smart for that."

He lets out a long sigh. "Here's the deal. I've been tasked with reconnaissance. Haven knows you haven't been going to the library the last week, and she wants to know why, but she's convinced if she's the one to ask you, you won't give her a straight answer. So, she's having me reach out and ask because she thinks you'll tell me the truth. Of course, I wasn't supposed to tell you all that, so keep that our little secret, yeah?"

"Ooooh, snitch." I let out a bark of laughter. "What does she suspect?"

"That you and Marie had an argument and you're avoiding her now."

Damn… Haven is way too perceptive for her own good. Marie probably talked to her—those two tell each other everything. Did she tell Haven about the kiss? I can only imagine the crazy ideas filling my sister's head right now.

"Nothing happened," I tell him. "I just have been taking up enough of her time at her job, so I thought I'd give her a break."

Christian snorts. "Right, okay. If that's the story you want to go with."

"Look, it just wasn't working for me to study at the library anymore," I say. It's not a lie; I'm just omitting the details of why it wasn't working anymore. "It's more convenient to do it on my own at home."

Christian lets out a skeptical humming sound. "It's really none of my business where you study and why, but I just want to make sure you're not making things more difficult for yourself because you're being stubborn."

The man knows me well.

"You tell Haven I'm fine," I reply. "She doesn't need to worry about me."

"Hmmm, all right, I'll tell her that. I can't guarantee she'll believe it, so she'll probably grill you later herself."

I shake my head and sigh. "Haven needs to just chill and focus on herself and the baby."

"Preaching to the choir, brother. You know you can tell me if there's anything wrong, right? You don't have to be all brave and tough for my sake."

"I know, man. Don't worry. If anything were really wrong, I'd tell you."

He sighs. "Okay. I'll give Haven an update, and hopefully, she'll let it go for now."

I doubt that, especially if Marie is upset about how things are between us.

"Thanks," I say. "I'll talk to you later."

We end the call, and I let out a long breath. This is getting too damn complicated. I need to figure out what to do about Marie. She's got me so torn up inside and wish I could talk to Mom. Get some advice and some guidance. Rubbing a hand across my chest, I feel an ache, as if my heart is twisting with my guilt and confusion.

Thinking of Mom makes me want to visit her. Maybe going to her grave and just being near her will help me clear my head. It sounds a little silly, but the thought fills me with a sudden yearning. I haven't been to her grave since the funeral. It's been in the back of my mind to do so, but I just haven't done it yet. It could make me feel better, at the very least.

With that decided, I clean up my notebooks and close my laptop, then go into my room to change my clothes. I'm not about to visit Mom in worn out sweatpants and a faded old t-shirt. Putting on jeans and a button-up, I check my reflection in my bathroom to make sure my hair isn't a mess, wanting to look my best for Mom.

When I'm ready, I grab my keys and head out to my truck. My heart is hammering, and I feel a strange burst of anxiety as I drive to the cemetery. I'm weirdly nervous about this, but I tell myself there's nothing to be nervous about.

I pass the flower shop downtown and the thought strikes me that I should take a bouquet with me. Pulling into a parking spot outside of the stop, I hop out and make my way inside. A few minutes later, I leave the shop with a bundle of brightly colored daffodils and daisies. They're cheery and pretty, just like Mom.

Climbing back into my truck, I continue on to the cemetery, my mind jumping between the two points of my struggle—my desire for Marie, and my promise to Mom. I feel like I can't acknowledge one without betraying the other. I also know I can't continue in this confusing haze of guilt.

Reaching the cemetery, I drive down the little dirt road, cutting through the collection of tombstones toward the area where my mother is buried. It's a peaceful place, surrounded by trees and dotted with bright flowers and displays around the graves from friends and family wanting to leave something for their loved one. There's a long row of American flags lined up toward the back of the cemetery with the names of the veterans laid to rest here. As far as I can tell, no one else is here right now.

Then I crest the hill that leads to Mom's spot, and to my surprise, I find a familiar car already parked at the end of the row where she's at. I stop the truck and frown, my stomach flipping.

I'd recognize that car anywhere... it's Marie's.

CHAPTER ELEVEN

MARIE

The sun warms my back as I kneel before Leila Merritt's grave, the bouquet of fresh daisies trembling in my hands. The cemetery is quiet, the kind of stillness that wraps itself around you and doesn't let go. It's peaceful, I suppose, but that peace only amplifies the guilt and sadness gnawing at my chest.

I set the flowers down gently, smoothing the ribbon around their stems.

"Hi, Leila," I whisper, my voice catching on her name. "It's been a while. I'm sorry I didn't come sooner."

The lump in my throat grows as I trace the engraving on the headstone: **Leila Merritt, Beloved Wife, Mother, and Friend.** If there was ever someone who embodied those words, it was her. She wasn't just a friend to me—she was so much more. After my mom passed, Leila stepped into that role with open arms, never making me feel like a burden, never treating me like the awkward outsider I felt I was at home.

I sit back on my heels, letting out a shaky breath.

"I'm sorry," I whisper. "I should've been there that weekend. I should've..." The words stick in my throat. "I wasn't there to say goodbye, and it's one of the biggest regrets of my life. I should've said no to Dad and Meredith. They wanted to go on a stupid weekend getaway, and I had to watch the kids. I was so angry because they knew you were sick and how much I wanted to be there in case you passed. They just didn't care, and I didn't push back when they guilted me into doing what they wanted. I should've been there for you, like you always were for me."

I'd known Leila was dying, that she could go at any time, but when my dad and stepmom - mostly stepmom and Dad giving into her every whim - guilted me into babysitting my youngest siblings so they could go away for the weekend, I'd convinced myself it was fine. That Leila would still be here when I was free to visit her one last time.

She wasn't.

"If I'm honest, it's not completely their faults," I murmur. "I couldn't face your death. Couldn't handle it. I avoided it as much as I could, and that was such a shitty thing to do. I'd lost my mom, and I didn't think I could handle losing you too. I wish I could go back," I choke, my fingers brushing against the cool stone. "I wish I could tell you how much you meant to me, how much you *still* mean to me."

Leila had never once treated me like an afterthought, unlike Meredith, who only ever sees me as an obligation. Leila listened when I needed to talk, hugged me when I felt like breaking, and cheered me on when I couldn't even cheer for myself. She gave me a place to belong when I didn't have one. Opened her home and her family to me. She didn't have to. Even though she'd been friends with my mom, Leila had been under no obligation to give a shit about me.

Yet, she did. I was able to have a somewhat normal childhood because of her, and I could spend almost every day with my best friend. Leila made losing my mom easier to deal with. When I was a teenager and needed a female figure to guide me through those tumultuous years to adulthood, Leila was that guide, not Meredith. When I was with Leila, I never doubted that she loved me. That her whole family did.

"You were more of a real mom to me," I admit. "More than Meredith could ever be, and I... I miss you every single day."

I wipe my cheeks quickly as the tears keep coming, my breath hitching in quick gasps. Suddenly, I hear footsteps crunching on the gravel behind me. My heart skips a beat, and I turn, startled.

It's Garrett.

He's standing there, tall and broad, with his familiar guarded expression that softens when his eyes meet mine. He's holding a bouquet of brightly colored flowers. The sight of him here, of all places, leaves me speechless. I haven't seen him in nearly a week—not since our kiss. My heart races, and I swallow, nervous. Is he going to run away again?

"I didn't mean to interrupt," he says, his voice low and steady.

I stand quickly, brushing off the grass from my knees and wiping at my eyes.

"You're not interrupting," I stammer, even though my face is probably blotchy and red. "I—I didn't know you'd be here. Sorry... I mean, I didn't know anyone would be here. I wouldn't have come... or, rather, I would have, but..."

Oh, God, I'm rambling. Why can't I keep it together around him? I wish I'd been more prepared to see him again, but being caught off guard like this is making my brain spin and my thoughts race. His gaze drifts to Leila's headstone, and I feel exposed somehow, like he's glimpsing something I didn't intend to share.

"Came to see Mom," he says simply, lifting the flowers slightly as if to explain.

Of course. Leila's his mom, after all, not mine. He has way more of a right to be here than I do. I feel like I'm intruding or am somewhere I shouldn't be. I take a shaky breath and gesture toward the gravestone.

"I was just visiting Leila... didn't mean to get in the way at all. I just needed to... to talk to her." My voice falters, and I look away, embarrassed by how raw my emotions are.

"You don't have to apologize for that," Garrett says softly, and when I glance at him, his eyes are full of kindness and he's smiling gently. "I know how important she was to you. You're allowed to miss her, and you're definitely allowed to visit her whenever you want. You don't need my permission."

Something about the way he says it, steady and unjudging, loosens the knot in my chest.

I nod, wiping at my eyes again. "Thanks."

He crouches in front of the headstone, setting the bouquet—daffodils and daisies, her favorite—down with a kind of reverence that makes my heart ache. He says nothing, just lingers there, his broad shoulders taut. After a moment, he rises, turning back to me with his usual no-nonsense expression, but there's a gentleness in his eyes that helps me relax.

"You wanna get a drink?" he asks suddenly, his voice breaking the stillness.

I blink, surprised. "A drink?"

He shrugs. "Yeah. Something to take the edge off. You look like you could use it."

I could use one. More than that, I could use the company. I'm so emotionally worn down, I just need to be around someone—anyone—even if it's Garrett.

Right now, I don't care about how tense and uncertain things have been between us. I just want to forget about what happened. About the kiss and him running away afterward. Right now, I'm emotional and need a friend. If he's willing to be that friend, who am I to turn him down?

I can't help but laugh softly, the sound surprising even me.

"I probably could. Are you sure you're not the one who needs it, though?"

His lips twitch into the faintest hint of a smile. "Maybe we both do."

"Fair enough," I say, brushing off my jeans and stepping toward the path. "Let's go."

We walk side by side; the gravel crunching underfoot as the breeze carries the scent of earth and flowers. It's a quiet, unhurried walk, but it doesn't feel awkward. For once, the silence is companionable, a shared time of reflection between two people who have both lost something.

When we reach the parking lot, Garrett pauses and looks at me.

"Do you want me to drive you?" he asks.

I shake my head. "How about this—I'll drive back to my place and walk to *Carson's*. It's not far."

"All right," he says. "I'll meet you there."

He waits until I'm in my car before he climbs into his truck. The low hum of my car engine fills the quiet space as I pull out of the cemetery. The gravel crunches beneath the tires, a sharp contrast to the soft whispers of wind through the trees just moments ago. My hands grip the steering wheel a little tighter than necessary as I think about my situation with Garrett now that I'm away from the cemetery and Leila's grave.

We don't see each other for days because he's trying so hard to avoid me, but now he wants to get a drink? I don't think I've ever gotten a drink with just Garrett before. We've always had Haven, and more recently Christian, acting as buffers for us. It's kind of funny. This is what I've always wanted—to be out, alone, with Garrett—and yet anxiety is bubbling in my stomach. This isn't even a date... right?

No, it's not a date. I need to get that thought of my head right the fuck now.

The car jerks slightly as I hit a pothole, pulling me back to the present. I drive downtown, passing the bar and my mother's store—my store. When I reach my house at the end of the street, I pull into the driveway and turn off the engine. I just sit there, staring at the steering wheel. At length, I sigh, grab my purse and step out into the crisp air, locking the car behind me.

The cool air bites at my cheeks as I make my way downtown. It's quiet out, just a few cars passing here and there. The faint glow of the bar's neon sign comes into view, and I feel a strange mix of nerves and anticipation.

I reach the bar a few minutes later and pause outside the door. Garrett's truck is already parked in the lot. This isn't a big deal. Just a quick drink with a friend. I'm not even going to think about our kiss... or how badly I want to do it again.

Shaking my head, I banish the thought. Lifting my chin, I plaster on a smile, reach out to open the door, and make my way inside.

CHAPTER TWELVE
GARRETT

When Marie walks in the door of *Carson's*, I raise my good arm and wave her over. I'm sitting in a booth in the corner, where we can have a modicum of privacy. She makes her way over to me and slips into the booth across from me. I push one of the two beers in front of me across the table to her. She takes it with a small smile.

"Thanks," she says before taking a drink.

Sitting back, I study her before asking, "Why were you visiting Mom today?"

She looks up at me, her expression hesitant. Maybe that question was too personal, but I can't help my curiosity.

Letting out a soft sigh, she answers, "I just need some clarity on a few things, and I thought going to her gravesite would help."

It's the same reason I was going there myself, but I don't say so. Still, I wonder what it is she needs clarity about—does it have to do with our kiss? Most likely, but again, I don't mention it. A part of me still isn't sure how to address that.

"I didn't know my mom's death hit you that hard," I say in a low voice. Obviously, I knew she was close to Mom, but what I saw out there in the cemetery was a display of grief as deep as my own.

Marie lifts her eyes to mine, her lashes glistening faintly in the muted light. "She meant a lot to me," she says softly. "More than I think you realize."

I frown, leaning forward and resting my elbows on the table. "What do you mean?"

She hesitates, her fingers tightening around the glass now. "You were older, Garrett. You had your own life. College, the oil fields... you didn't see how much she did for me when I was a teenager. Just how she was with me when I was younger."

I sit back, Marie's words settling over me. She's ten years younger than me. By the time she and Haven were in high school, I was long out of the house.

"I guess I didn't," I admit. "Want to tell me what all she did?"

Marie exhales, a sad smile curving her lips. "After my mom passed... it was hard, but I was so young it didn't fully sink in until I got older. Dad remarried when I was nine, and, as you know, Meredith didn't exactly roll out the welcome mat for me. Your mom... she saw that. She'd invite me over even when Haven didn't. Bake cookies and ask about school. Hug me when I had a bad day, and I didn't have anyone else to talk to. She taught me how to be a woman—gave me the talk, explained periods, showed me how to do my makeup and hair."

Her voice cracks a little, and I feel like someone's tightened a vise around my chest.

"Marie..." I start, but she shakes her head, cutting me off.

"It's okay. I'm just trying to explain. She wasn't just your mom, Garrett. She was mine, too, in a way."

Sadness and vulnerability lace into her voice, causing my heart to hurt. I've always thought of Marie as this fiercely independent woman who lets nothing or anyone get to her. Knowing she leaned on my mom in such intimate, vital ways....

Marie's smile turns bitter. "My family is so fucking complicated." She tightens her grip on her beer, not looking at me. "I love my siblings. I really do. But Meredith? I can't stand her. She's always treated me like an outsider. And Dad... I don't know. He's just abandoned me in favor of his new family."

The words come out fast, like she's just been waiting for a chance to spill all this.

She takes a breath before adding, "I miss having a mom every day. I missed out on so much growing up without mine. If it weren't for your family—for Laila—I don't know how I would've made it through. Without her, I would've been utterly... alone."

My stomach twists at her raw vulnerability. Marie never talks like this... not to me, at least. She's laying it all out for me, and I'm not sure what to say to make it better.

"You're not alone," I manage, my voice rough. "You've got Haven and me."

Her eyes snap to mine, wide and searching. For what, I'm not sure.

"Do I?" she whispers.

The question makes my heart hammer. I've always thought of Marie as Haven's best friend. She's just always been there. A fixture in our lives. Have I ever made her feel like an outsider? Like she doesn't belong with us?

"Yeah," I say firmly. "You do."

Marie looks at me, and I can see doubt easing from her expression. She reaches for her drink again, taking a small sip before setting it down with a soft thud. Did I say something wrong? Why does she doubt that I'll be there for her? My heart aches and I want to assure her that, no matter what, I'm not going to stop caring for her.

"Hey." I reach across the table and grab her hand, giving it a reassuring squeeze. "You *do*. Haven and I will always be here for you. I promise."

She stares at me, and her expression softens as relief brightens her gaze.

"Thanks," she breathes, her lips curving into a faint smile. "That means a lot."

The evening stretches on after that, and Marie and I fall into a comfortable rhythm, talking about school, work, and more general topics that are light and easy. She's been open enough with me tonight, and I don't want to push her any further. I want to make her smile again and help her relax.

"You've got a way of making everything sound like it's not such a big deal," she says at one point, her eyes shimmering and her lips curled into a grin. She's moved closer to me, slipping around the U-shaped booth to sit on my side.

Chuckling, I shake my head. "I think you give me too much credit. I just don't let things bother me for too long."

She presses her shoulder against my good one. "I could learn a thing or two from you."

"Maybe," I say softly. "But I think I could learn a thing or two from you, too."

She blinks up at me; her plump lips parting in surprise. "You think so?"

I nod. I can't help myself, I reach up and brush my thumb along her chin. Her eyelids flutter and she leans into my touch. I swallow. This is dangerous. We're playing with fire right now, but I can't seem to resist.

The bar quiets down while the bartender stacks empty glasses as the last few patrons filter out. We continue to stare at each other in silence, oblivious to the room around us.

"I should probably go home," she murmurs.

"I'll walk you."

She raises an eyebrow, but doesn't protest. We stand and make our way out of the bar into the cool night. Side by side we walk, the quiet hum of the town surrounding us, the streets empty save for the occasional car passing by. We don't talk, just let the tension sizzle between us, the sound of our footsteps mingling with the faint rustling of leaves in the breeze.

We pass by the old boutique that Marie's mom left her. It's closed now, but I can't help but notice how her eyes linger on it. She always used to talk about opening it as a bookshop, and was so excited by the idea. The past few years, though, she's talked about it less and less.

"Still thinking about the shop?" I ask, trying to keep my voice casual, but there's an edge to it.

Marie shrugs. "I don't know. I've got so many plans. So many things I want to do with it, but I don't know if any of it's going to happen."

I slow my pace a little. "What do you mean?"

She glances over at me but quickly looks away.

"I don't want to talk about it right now, okay?" The words come out soft, almost like a plea, and I don't press her further. I'm burning with curiosity. What's holding her back from opening the shop again if that's what she wants?

"Alright," I say quietly, matching her pace as we continue walking.

When we reach her house, she turns to face me, her cheeks flushed.

"Thanks for walking me home," she says.

"No problem."

The tension is palpable now. I can feel the heat of her, the way her eyes don't quite meet mine, but linger just long enough for my heart to race.

She hesitates, then says, "You want to come inside for a bit?"

I swallow hard, the question hanging in the air like a dare—a temptation. It's an invitation, plain and simple, but I know she's not asking me in for a nightcap. A little voice in my head says I should leave. Tell her goodnight, turn around, and walk away before I do something I might regret.

However, an even louder voice urges me to go inside with her. To see where exactly this leads.

"Sure," I say at length.

She gives me a small, almost shy smile and leads me to her front door. I stand behind her as she unlocks and opens it. Once we're inside with the door closed again, I grab her hand and turn her around to face me. Her eyes go wide as she stares up at me and I cup the side of her face.

"Garrett..." she murmurs.

I cut her off, pressing my lips to hers in a gentle kiss. I take my time, handling her with care as I brush my fingertips across her cheek. She whimpers and wraps her arms around my neck, pressing her body tight against mine. I keep the pace slow, though. We're both so emotionally raw and vulnerable, I don't want to push too hard too fast.

Our tongues meet and explore as I reach down, cupping her ass and picking her up off the floor. Her legs wind around my waist and we continue to kiss as I walk through her house and make my way upstairs to her bedroom. The mixture of alcohol and desire heats my body and banishes away all hesitations and reservations I've been holding onto, and all I can think about is how good she tastes and how right she feels in my arms.

When we reach her bedroom, I set her back down and pull from our kiss. She gazes up at me, her eyes hooded and lips swollen from our kiss.

"I want you," she says. "I want you more than anything."

I take her face in both my hands and reply, "I want you too. More than I should."

She frowns at that, but before she can say anything in

response, I kiss her again. Reaching down, I grab the hem of her shirt and pull it up and over her head, tossing it aside. Her fingers fumble with the buttons of my shirt, and I help her undo them before shrugging out of it. Grabbing her waist, I pull her back against my body and kiss her like a starving man who's been given a banquet.

I walk her backward to the bed and set her down on the edge of the mattress. Kneeling before her, I gaze up at her as I undo her jeans and tug them down her legs. She's breathing heavily, her breasts moving up and down and nearly spilling out of her bra.

"What are you doing?" she asks, her voice breathy. I lift one of her legs and kiss the inside of her ankle and slowly move my way up her calf to her inner thigh.

"I'm going to have a taste," I tell her, reaching for her panties.

She gasps and I tug her panties down her legs. Grasping her thighs, I push her legs apart and gaze down at her glistening sex.

"Fuck," I growl. "You're already so wet."

"You have that effect on me," she pants.

Chuckling, I smirk at her before lowering my head and dragging my tongue along her folds. She lets out a needy cry and grabs hold of my hair. I hold her in place as I lick and suck on her tender flesh, savoring her honey and every tremble of her body. God, she tastes better than I imagined. I could grow addicted to this... to her. How was I able to resist this for so long?

"Oh, my God," she moans.

When I wrap my lips around her clit and suck, she jerks and squeals. I hold on to her tighter so she can't get away from me.

"Garrett," she whimpers. "Please... I need more."

Fucking music to my ears, but I want to make her come like this first. I lick and suck harder and within moments, her thighs clench around my head and she's crying out, clutching at the sheets on either side of her. I draw out her orgasm for as long as I can until she pushes at my head and wiggles to get out of my grasp.

Chuckling, I stand and gaze down at her as I undo my jeans and push them down my legs, releasing my throbbing cock. Marie's eyes go wide and her lips curl into a hungry grin.

"Like what you see?" I ask.

She nods. "Very much."

Her legs fall open further in invitation, and she crooks her finger at me. Growling, I climb onto the bed and settle between her legs. Staring down at her, I take a second to let this situation really sink in. This is happening. I'm about to cross this line with Marie, and there's no going back. Right now, though, I don't care. I don't want to go back. I want to watch her fall apart from the pleasure I give her, and I want to lose myself in her soft, luscious body.

Sliding her hands up my arms, she grips my forearms.

"I want you inside me," she whispers.

What man could resist such a sweet invitation like that? Not me, that's for damn sure. I grab a condom from my wallet and drag it down my length. Lining my shaft up with her entrance, I press forward, entering her in one swift thrust of my hips.

Marie throws her head back with a cry. Bracing my arms on either side of her head, I capture her lips in a hard kiss as I move. In and out, in and out. She clings to me and I catch her moans and cries with my kiss.

It's so good. She feels so perfect—wet and tight and greedy. Pleasure washes over me and I grow lost in her. We move together, our hips meeting and grinding as we both desperately chase our release. Reaching between us, I press my thumb to her clit and rub it in tight circles.

"Come for me, baby," I rasp. "I want to feel you coming around my cock."

She squirms and whines as I push her to the edge. Lifting my head, I watch as she hits her peak. Her eyes go wide and her mouth falls open on a silent cry as her back arches off the bed. She digs her nails into my shoulders and the pain only enhances my pleasure. Her pussy spasms around me and squeezes me like it doesn't want to let me go.

It's too much. I can't hold myself back and bury my face in her neck as my orgasm rips through me. I ride it out, pumping my hips in and out of her until my body shudders and my vision wavers while her body jerks beneath me. Reaching a point where I can't hold myself up any longer, I collapse but am careful to fall to the side so I don't crush her under my weight.

The room is silent except for our heaving breaths. That was so... intense. I've never experienced so much pleasure with someone before. I turn my head to look at her and find her gazing at me with a soft smile.

"Shit," she says. "That was... incredible."

"Yeah, it really was."

Rolling to her side, she snuggles closer to me and rests her head on my chest.

"Don't leave," she whispers. "Stay like this with me. Please."

Wrapping my arms around her, I hold her tight and stare up at the ceiling without saying a word. I'll stay with her like this for the night, but in the back of my mind I know that once the sun rises, I'll have to face the consequences of this night, and the guilt that's already twisting in my belly.

CHAPTER THIRTEEN
MARIE

The morning light filters through the curtains, soft and golden, and I blink awake, warmth still clinging to my skin. I feel a sleepy contentment, the kind that makes you want to burrow back into the blankets and savor it. Then I reach across the bed, expecting to feel Garrett beside me.

The sheets are cold.

My heart sinks. I push myself up on one elbow, scanning the room. His clothes are gone, his boots missing from where they'd been kicked off near the door. He's not here.

I lay back down, staring at the ceiling, trying to push away the ache building in my chest. He left without a word.

I shouldn't feel this way—I knew what we were doing last night. It wasn't like either of us made promises or talked about what it meant. Still, there's this hollow feeling I can't ignore, a creeping fear that maybe I overestimated how much last night mattered to him. Maybe I let myself hope a little too much that we were finally turning a corner together.

I grab my phone from the nightstand and type out a quick text.

> Marie: Hey. Just wanted to check in. Did you get home okay?

I hesitate before hitting send, wondering if it sounds too needy. What else am I supposed to say? After a few seconds of agonizing indecision, I send it.

The message delivers. I wait a few minutes, but no reply comes.

I sigh, tossing my phone onto the bed and forcing myself to get up. There's no use sitting here overthinking. I have to go to work, and if nothing else, maybe the routine of my day will distract me.

The morning drags as I shower, throw on a dress, and try to make myself look halfway put together. My reflection in the mirror doesn't help. My hair feels impossible to tame, and there's a tired look in my eyes I can't seem to blink away.

"Pull yourself together, Marie," I mutter to myself.

At the library, I go through the motions—unlocking the doors, turning on the lights, straightening shelves, and logging into the system. It's usually my favorite part of the day, the quiet time before anyone comes in, when the world feels calm. Today, it just feels empty. Part of me hopes Garrett will show up. That he'll come in and give me a logical reason for leaving so early and not responding to my text. Then, he'll kiss me and ask me out to dinner.

But the hours tick by, and there's no sign of him.

By lunchtime, I'm restless. My mind stuck replaying last night and the way he looked at me, the way he touched me like I mattered, like he couldn't get close enough. The pleasure we shared and the feel of his arms around me as I cuddled against his chest and fell asleep listening to his heartbeat. Was it all just in my head?

I pull out my phone again and check for a reply to my text.

Nothing. The disappointment hits me harder than I want to admit.

"Marie? Are you okay, dear?"

Startled, I find Kathy watching me, her brow furrowed in concern.

Swallowing, I quickly reply, "Yeah, I'm fine."

She frowns and shakes her head. "You've been preoccupied all day. Something's on your mind."

I force a reassuring smile and insist, "Really, I'm all good. You don't have to worry."

Kathy still doesn't appear convinced. She gazes around, as if looking for something, or someone, and then focuses back on me.

"It's been so long since Garrett has been by," she says at length. "Where's he been hiding?"

Sucking in a breath, I tense, feeling as if she's able to see straight through me. Clearing my throat, I reply, "I think he's just been busy, that's all."

Kathy regards me for several moments, and I'm afraid she's going to press me for a better answer. I don't know what to tell her. Honestly, I don't know what's going on with Garrett. How do I explain that every time we have a physical encounter, he disappears on me? First our kiss, then last night. He's just... gone. As if he thinks he can run from the intimacy we've shared.

Instead of digging further, Kathy says, "If there's one thing I've learned in all my years, Marie, it's that you can't give up on anything or anyone you truly care about. Life is far too short not to grab onto what you want with both hands and hang on to it with all your strength. It can take some time, but you just have to keep fighting. You don't want to live with any regrets."

I blink, taken aback by her sudden advice.

"O...okay," I stammer, unsure what else I should say.

She gives me a soft smile and turns back to her work,

checking returned books back into the system. I just sit and watch her for several seconds before focusing back on my own work. Her words continue to play inside my mind, though, and I can't help but wonder if she's right. If Garrett is the man I really want, how long am I willing to keep fighting for him?

KATHY'S ADVICE stays at the forefront of my mind until the end of the day. When I leave the library to head home, I still have no idea what I'm going to do about Garrett, but I can't deny that my feelings for him are as strong as ever.

I'm so lost in thought that I make my way home by muscle memory alone, and I don't realize there's someone waiting for me on my front porch steps until I'm nearly on top of him.

"Garrett!" I exclaim in shock, nearly jumping out of my skin. "What are you doing here?"

He's sitting on the top step, wearing dark jeans and a brown leather jacket. His elbows are resting on his knees and he looks like he's been waiting here for a little bit.

Clearing his throat, he pushes to his feet and I have to tilt my head back to maintain eye contact.

"Hey, Marie," he begins in a stiff tone. "I, uh, wanted to come by and apologize to you."

"Apologize?" I frown, confused. "For what?"

He rubs the back of his neck, looking tense and uncomfortable.

"What happened last night was a mistake," he says with a sigh. "I shouldn't have let it happen, and I'm sorry."

My heart sinks and disappointment settles on my shoulders like a weighted blanket. I drop my gaze from his and take a moment to collect myself. I don't want to break right now. Not until I've said what I need to say.

"I don't think it was a mistake," I reply softly.

"I shouldn't have crossed that line with you," he continues, as if I haven't spoken. "You're like a sister to me, Marie, and it wasn't right of me to take advantage of you like I did. You were vulnerable. We'd both been drinking... I should have walked away."

Jerking my gaze back up to his, I stare at him, dumbfounded. Seriously? *This* is what he wants to say to me right now?

"You didn't take advantage of me." Frustration bubbles up inside of me. Once again, he's treating me with kid gloves, and that's not something I've ever wanted from him. "I was a very willing participant and knew exactly what I was doing. I'm a grown-ass woman, Garrett! I'm not a child, so I'd appreciate it if you didn't treat me like one."

His eyes go wide and he stares at me, clearly stunned. What? Shocked that I'm actually calling him on his bullshit for once?

"I know you're not a child," he says at length, his tone low and firm. "Regardless, what happened last night can't happen again."

"Why?" I demand to know. I'm so sick of this. So sick of him dodging me and giving me these lame, half-assed reasons for not giving me a chance. "Why can't it happen again? And don't you dare tell me it's because you think of me like a sister, because I know that's bullshit. None of this would've happened at all if that was true."

He clenches his jaw and frustration flashes through his gaze. Good! I'm actually getting some emotion out of him!

"I care about you, Marie," he grumbles at last. "I always will, and I'll always be there for you... as a friend. But it can't be anything more than that."

"Not good enough," I hiss, balling my hands into fists at my sides, struggling not to beat them against his chest in frustration.

His eyes narrow. "Well, it's all you're going to get."

With that, he moves past me and storms away. I watch him go, stunned by his easy dismissal. Son of a bitch!

Tears prick the corners of my eyes and I whirl back around and hurry up my porch steps to my front door, overwhelmed by disappointment and heartbreak. Once inside, I slam my door shut as hard as I can to get the last word in, so to speak, and I hope he hears it and knows how much he's hurt me.

CHAPTER FOURTEEN
GARRETT

Coming back to the library might have been a mistake. It's been three weeks since my fight with Marie in front of her house. I hurt her feelings that night, and I have no idea how to fix things between us. She was angry that night, but also disappointed, her emotions bright in her eyes. I decided to return to the library to try and start mending things between us, but in the couple days I've been back, she hasn't spoken to me, all but ignoring me.

It hasn't been the same. Not by a longshot. Every time I come in now, she claims she has too much work to do and can't help me one-on-one like before. Instead, she has Ally sit with me and help me with my homework. It's obvious she's trying to keep her distance, and it's a gut-punch every time. I'm doing well in my class and am close to getting the last few credits I need to earn my degree, and it's all because of Marie.

I'm also mostly healed, except for a few more physical therapy sessions for my shoulder. I should be a lot happier than I am—celebrating and looking forward to starting the next chapter of my life. I'm not happy. Not while Marie is so upset with me.

"Hey, Garrett? Earth to Garrett! Helloooo, have you been listening?"

Ally watches me with an amused grin. We're sitting at a computer near the front desk of the library, where Marie works intently, appearing to do her best not to look our way at all.

"Huh?" I blink. "Oh! Yeah, uh, sorry... what were you saying?"

She arches her brow. "Whatcha looking at?"

Scowling, I say, "Nothing, what are you talking about?"

"Oh, geez." She rolls her eyes and groans. "You're being so ridiculous. Both of you are."

I frown at her, but before I can ask her what she means, a large figure enters the library. When I recognize Mason Rowland, a childhood friend who'd recently moved back to town to set up his contracting business, I can't help my surprise. What's he doing here? The library isn't really a place I'd expect to find him.

Briefly, I wonder if he's here for Marie. He used to have a thing for her back in the day—he had a thing for a lot of girls— and he was always charming and able to sweep them off their feet. What if he tries that with Marie? Jealousy and frustration burn through me, but Mason walks right on by the front desk. He's looking around, as if searching, and when his eyes land on me, he grins and waves.

"There you are!" he declares, strolling right up to my desk. "Haven thought you'd be here."

"Hey, Mason," I reply, standing and giving him a back slapping hug. "You've been looking for me?"

He returns the hug and then steps back and gives me a once over. Arching his brow, he gives me an amused grin. "I tried calling a few days ago, but you never got back to me. Pure coincidence that I was passing the library and saw you through the windows." He chuckles. "I didn't peg you for a bookworm."

"Yeah, not usually, but I'm working on finishing my degree. Being here helps me focus."

Or, it used to. Not so much anymore.

"Impressive," Mason says. "You need a break? I wanted to see if you were up for hanging out with me tonight. It's been so long since we've gone out and partied together. I thought it'd be fun—relive the glory days a bit."

Chuckling, I shake my head. "I don't know if I can survive reliving our glory days, man."

"Ah, come on!" Mason urges. "I've been so busy since moving back that I haven't had any time to hang with you!"

"It's good to see you," I assure him. "But, I'm just not sure..." I catch Marie's gaze over Mason's shoulder. She's watching us, with pursed lips and furrowed brows. She doesn't look happy and, she quickly jerks her gaze away and pretends to be busy. My heart sinks at her blatant attempt to ignore me. I look back to Mason and say, "Actually, you know what? A night out might be just what I need. The distraction could be good. I'm in."

"Great," Mason grins. "I'll text you where, but shoot for a meeting at eight?"

"Sounds like a plan."

Mason leaves shortly after that, and as he goes, I look back over to Marie. She has her head down, seemingly focused on something in front of her, but her jaw is clenched and her cheeks are red. Taking a deep breath, I cross to her and stand in front of the desk.

"Hey, um, Marie," I begin. "Can we talk...?"

"Sorry, I can't," she says in a short tone, not bothering to glance up at me. "Too busy."

"Look, I just want to clear the air..."

"Nothing to clear," she snaps, gathering up a pile of books. "I need to get back to work."

She turns and walks away into the back room, leaving me staring after her in stunned silence.

Fuck.

Sighing, I sit back down in my chair and try to focus on my work. Ally is shaking her head with an irritated expression.

"Ridiculous," she grumbles.

I don't bother to ask her what she means.

CARSON'S IS BUSY, which isn't a surprise for a Friday night. Other roughnecks enjoy their time away from the fields. A few townies unwind after a long week, and plenty of girls mill around, laughing and flirting as they convince guys to buy them drinks. It's the typical scene for this place on the weekends, and when I was younger, it'd be just what I'd need to unwind and have some fun.

As I settle at a table with Mason, a bottle of beer in my hand, I'm not as interested in being here. I want to hang out with Mason, sure, but I'm just not in the mood to deal with other people. The image of Marie's face after Mason left the library earlier won't leave my head and I feel oddly... guilty.

"Hey, man, you good?" Mason asks, pulling me from my gloomy thoughts.

I meet his gaze, forcing a smile. "Yeah, no worries. Just got lost in my head for a bit."

Mason furrows his brow. "You've been through a lot lately, huh? I was sorry to hear about your mom."

"Thanks," I say softly. "That was tough, but she's not in pain anymore, so that's something to be grateful for."

"Absolutely."

We chat for a bit, catching up. Mason gives me the rundown

of his new business and what it's like moving back to Blue Ridge Falls after being away for so long. His family moved at the end of our sophomore year of high school, but he kept in touch and visited throughout the years, so his connection to the town remained strong.

As we're talking, a couple girls start to circle us, flashing us smiles as they try to catch our attention. A tall brunette and a curvy blonde, both in short skirts and flannel shirts over low-cut tank-tops. I vaguely recognize them from around town, but I can't place their names. When Mason finally notices them, he grins and waves them over.

"Hey, there," he greets as they approach our table. Looking back at me, he says, "Garrett, do you know Bailey and Kate? I just did some work at their boutique downtown."

"And we are in love with everything you did," the blonde—Bailey?—declares with a flirty smile. "We're so grateful for your hard work, Mason."

He clearly enjoys the attention. "It was my pleasure, beautiful."

The brunette, Kate, turns to me and bats her long lashes. "You're Haven's brother, right? My nephew is in her classroom at the daycare. He loves her."

I nod. "Yep, and I'm not surprised. Kids tend to adore her. She's a natural with them."

Kate saddles closer to me and flips her hair over her shoulder.

"Had I known she had such a handsome brother, I'd have insisted that she introduce us before now."

I'm not going to lie—her attention is flattering. I've been injured and focused on school for so long, my social life has all but died, and there's been very little interaction with women. I can barely remember the last time I had sex before Marie, which was something I never had a problem with getting before. Hook-ups were always my thing. I never got bogged down by emotions or the desire for more from a woman. It was never complicated for me.

Not until Marie.

Quickly shoving thoughts of her away, I curl my lips into what I know is a charming smile and say, "We're meeting now, so better late than never, right?"

She giggles and rests her hand on my arm. At the feel of her touch, an image of Marie naked and spread out beneath me flashes through my mind, her eyes hooded and dark with desire as she stares up at me. Just like that, any interest that might have been starting to sizzle for Kate vanishes.

Shit. What is wrong with me? A pretty girl is standing right next to me, making her interest obvious, but all I can think about is that she's not Marie.

Ally was right... I am ridiculous.

I do my best to keep talking and flirting with Kate, but my heart isn't in it. When she and Bailey slip away to the bathroom together, I seize the chance to get out of here.

"Hey, Mason, I'm going to head out," I say, trying to sound nonchalant.

He frowns. "What? Already? You sure? We can go somewhere else if you want to..."

"Nah, I'm good. I need to get up early to get some schoolwork done. You stay and have fun, and apologize to Kate for me, all right?"

Mason sighs, looking disappointed. "Yeah, all right. Have a good night, man."

"You too."

I grab my jacket and turn to head for the door, but before I even make two steps, it swings open. My jaw drops when Marie strolls inside with Maggie, who works at the daycare with Haven, in all her pink-haired glory next to her. They're both dressed for a night out in short dresses, and Marie looks gorgeous and sexy. Almost every guy in the bar turns to gaze at her, and I'm not fucking going anywhere.

CHAPTER FIFTEEN
MARIE

This was a mistake. I shouldn't have come here.

After our fight, I was so upset with Garrett that I could hardly look at him, let alone talk to him. He hurt me, and I still don't think he realizes how much. I managed to go three weeks without seeing him until he started showing back up at the library, but I just kept ignoring him. Then I overheard his conversation with Mason, and something in me snapped.

When I heard that Garrett was going out with his friend, I couldn't help myself. It wasn't fair that he could just move on as if our fight meant nothing...as if I meant nothing. If he could go out and have a good time, then I could too! I called up Maggie, knowing she'd be up for a night out. I'd known there was a chance he'd be at *Carson's*, because it's not like this town is crawling with bars, but I'd hoped he'd end up somewhere else so I could just enjoy my night out in relative peace.

I should've just stayed home and not risked it.

As he stares at me, slack jawed, a pretty brunette comes up beside him and grabs his arm, pulling him back to the table Mason is sitting at with a blonde.

Fuck, this was what I was afraid of. I remembered all the

stories I'd heard about Garrett and Mason's antics when they were in high school, especially the stories about all the girls they'd pursued. Looks like I was right to worry. It seems the guys are really revisiting their glory days, just like Mason said they would back in the library.

Part of me wants to turn around and leave, but Garrett's seen me. It'll be obvious that I'm running away because of him, and that would be so humiliating. Still, I don't know if I can stay and watch him flirt with other women. I'm frozen in place, uncertain whether I should move forward or back.

Maggie slips her arm through mine, and smiles up at me.

"Come on, let's get a drink," she says, winking.

Relief and gratitude wash through me at her willingness to step up and take charge right now.

"All right."

She gives my arm a squeeze and leads me through the crowd toward the bar. I do my best to ignore Garrett, but his eyes follow me from across the room.

When we reach the bar, Maggie waves the bartender over.

"Can we get a vodka soda, and... what do you want, Marie?"

"Oh, um, just a ginger ale."

She raises her brows in surprise. "You sure? It's on me."

Truth be told, I'd love a good strong drink, but I don't think my stomach can handle it. Just thinking about liquor has it twisting and the nausea I've been experiencing the last couple days bubbling back up.

I wince, but then smile and nod. "I'm sure, really."

Maggie shrugs. "All righty, one ginger ale it is."

The bartender brings out drinks and Maggie hands me mine.

"Cheers," I say, clinking my glass with hers.

She gives me a concerned look. "Are you okay?"

"I'm fine," I reply. "I've just had a bit of a stomach bug the last few days, so drinking probably isn't a good idea."

"That's not what I meant." She glances behind me, right at Garrett. It's no secret my feelings for him, but I didn't know it was so obvious. "If you want, we can dip out after this drink. It won't be weird that way."

I chuckle and give her an appreciative hand pat. "It's okay. We can stay here. I just want to relax and have some fun."

"We can do that, no problem," Maggie assures me.

We sip our drinks and chat and laugh, and I pretend I don't feel Garrett's gaze boring into me. Maggie has a few more vodka sodas and I have another ginger ale before she grabs my hand and tugs me off my stool.

"Let's dance!" she exclaims.

She drags me out to the crowded dance floor. She twirls me and I laugh, and as we dance, my stress and anxiety melts away. This is what I've needed. To just let loose and not think about anything, or anyone. Garrett's still there—I can sense him even if I do my best not to look in his direction—but I'm not letting his presence and those girls he's with keep me from enjoying myself.

A tall man in jeans and a button up black shirt slips through the crowd toward me. He's not bad-looking, with dark hair and brown eyes and he seems decently in shape. When he reaches me, he looks me up and down with an appreciative smile.

"Hey, beautiful," he says loud enough that I can hear him over the music. "Wanna dance?"

I'm not super interested, but maybe this is what I need. Attention from other men to help me finally get over my obsession with Garrett.

"Okay," I answer, taking his hand.

The guy immediately moves closer and puts his hands on my waist. Okay... that's all right, I guess. We start to dance, but the music suddenly changes into something slower. Before I can make an excuse to step away, he pulls me closer so I'm pressed tight against him.

"Um, I think I should find my friend..."

"Don't worry, baby," he murmurs with a hungry grin. "I'll take care of you."

His breath, hot on my neck, smells sharply of alcohol. It makes my stomach churn. Ew... this guy's getting real creepy, real fast.

"That's okay," I say, pushing against his chest. "I don't need to be taken care of."

His grip on me moves lower toward my ass.

"I like a girl who plays hard to get."

I push harder and scowl up at him. "Hey, I'm not kidding, and I'm not playing hard to get. I don't want to dance with you anymore. Let me go."

"Just relax, baby, and enjoy the ride..."

"I said no!"

Suddenly, a hand reaches past me and shoves the guy away.

"She said no."

Garrett's deep voice sends a shiver down my spine. He brings his other arm around my waist and pulls me back against him. I instantly feel more at ease pressed against his body. I'm safe now, and don't have to worry anymore.

The guy looks pissed, but he turns his gaze up and gets a good look at Garrett

"Whatever," he grumbles before turning and skulking away, disappearing back into the crowd.

Turning, I tilt my head back and meet Garrett's eyes. His expression is fierce, but it immediately softens when he looks down at me.

"You okay?" he asks.

I gulp, caught off guard by being so close to him so suddenly. "Um...I am. Thanks."

He takes my hand and pulls me close. "Wanna dance with me instead?"

My heart is racing and I hesitate, reminding myself that I'm still angry with him. He said some really hurtful things...yet the heat from his body is wrapping around me, and his bright green gaze is unwavering as he stares down at me. He has dark stubble along his jaw and his hair is a little wild, which really works for him. Damn it...why does he have to be so damn gorgeous?

"Sure," I murmur as he pulls me even closer.

Slipping my arms around his neck, we start to sway to the music. I can't lie... I'm confused. My feelings for Garrett are a jumbled mess, and I don't know what it means that he stepped in and saved me from that asshole. Was he just being a good friend? A good *brother*?

Or did he do it because he cares more about me than that? Did he not like seeing another man touching me?

I don't know, but right this second, I don't think I care. All that matters is that he's holding me, chasing off the bad guys, and making me feel cared for and safe.

Letting out a soft breath, I rest my head against his chest. Will he push me away?

He doesn't. In fact, he drops his chin onto the top of my head. The tension between us is thick, but neither of us address it. In fact, we don't say anything as we continue to dance.

When the song comes to an end and a more energetic one starts playing, Garrett and I stop. I don't want to walk away from him, but I don't know how to be around him anymore. My heart hurts remembering how he declared that our night together was a mistake when it meant so much to me. However, it also can't seem to let him go.

"Why don't I take you home?" he asks.

I frown, surprised by the offer. "What about Mason and... those girls? Won't they be upset if you ditch them?"

He chuckles softly and shakes his head. "No, they won't be. I was going to leave anyway before you walked in. Then I couldn't make myself go."

My heart races at that, but I try not to get ahead of myself and read too much into his words.

"Oh? What if I'm not ready to leave?"

He arches a brow. "You want to stay?"

I nibble my bottom lip before admitting, "No, I don't. I want to go home."

"Then I'll take you."

I put a hand on his chest. "I need to let Maggie know."

He nods. "All right."

Turning away from him, I search the dancefloor and spot Maggie. She's dancing with a cut blonde guy who seems entranced by her. I cross over to them, and Garrett follows close behind me. My chest flutters at his apparent protectiveness.

When I reach Maggie, I pat her on the shoulder to get her attention. She turns her head to me, blinking as if she's coming out of a daze.

"Marie! You okay?"

I lean in so I can speak directly into her ear. "I'm going to head out. Are you good?"

She gives me a thumbs up as the blonde guy hugs her tighter, as if he's afraid I'm going to steal her away.

"I'm good," she assures me. "You go ahead. I can see you've got an escort to make sure you get home safe."

She gazes pointedly over my shoulder, and I steal a glance back at Garrett. He's looking around the dance floor, like he's keeping an eye out for potential threats. It'd be funny if I hadn't just dealt with that awful creep.

I focus back on Maggie. "Yeah, he's going to walk me home. Text me when you get home later, okay?"

"I will, I promise."

Usually, I wouldn't feel good about leaving a friend alone in a bar, but Maggie is more than capable of taking care of herself. *Carson's* is one of her favorite haunts in town and she comes here by herself all the time. The owner knows her so well, he's always looking out for her.

Turning back to Garrett, I say, "Do you need to let Mason know?"

"No, we're good."

"Okay, then let's get out of here."

Garrett places his hand on my lower back and directs me away from the dance floor and toward the bar's front door. His palm feels hot, even through my clothes, and heat pools deep in my belly. No matter how confused my head and heart might be, my body knows exactly what it wants. It wants Garrett. The other man's touch repelled me, but Garetts' sets me on fire. I don't know if I'll ever have that with anyone else, and that possibility terrifies me.

What if he's ruined me for other men? What if I can never move on from him, even in the face of his rejection?

My heart races and I move more quickly to get to the door, suddenly needing air as the possibility of a life without Garrett —without anyone—crushes my chest and makes it difficult to breathe.

CHAPTER SIXTEEN
GARRETT

When we step out of the bar, the cool night air hits me, chilling the sweat along my forehead and the back of my neck. I shiver, but the cold is refreshing after the heat of the bar.

The streets are quiet, illuminated by the soft glow of the streetlights. It's a stark contrast from the crowded party atmosphere inside *Carson's*. It's peaceful and I feel like I can breathe properly for the first time in over an hour. Marie tilts her head back and sucks in a deep breath before slowly letting it out. Her shoulders relax and the tension around her jaw lessens.

"It's a nice night," she murmurs before turning to walk down the sidewalk. I walk beside her, hands shoved in my pockets. We don't talk for several moments and I'm not sure what to say. Instead, I steal glances her way and replay the scene in the bar over and over in my head.

She'd walked into the bar, looking so damn good in her little dress and her dark brown hair falling in soft curls around her shoulders. Her deep brown eyes had locked on me and I hadn't been able to look away from her, and the way her dress hugged her curves in all the right ways. Later, when I saw that asshole dancing with her—touching her—jealousy stole my breath. I'd had to fight not to storm over to them right that second and rip her from his arms. When it became obvious that she wanted to get away and he wasn't letting her, I'd let myself loose. If we hadn't been surrounded by witnesses, I'd have beaten that fucker's face into the floor.

"You should be more careful," I say.

She looks up at me with a frown. "What?"

"You shouldn't let random guys get so close to you. You can't be sure what they're intentions are."

She comes to an immediate stop and turns to me with a scowl, her eyes flashing with anger.

"That's none of your business," she snaps. "I appreciate you stepping in when you did, but that doesn't mean you get to criticize me and the way I interact with other men."

"Well, you clearly weren't thinking straight, letting that guy put his hands on you," I growl.

She lets out a frustrated groan and continues storming down the sidewalk. I hurry after her, not ready to let this issue go.

"I was having fun," she hisses. "It's not my fault if that shithead ended up being a creep. I'm not responsible for his actions."

"That just means you have to be more careful," I insist. "Yeah, it's not fair, I get that, but that's why you have to be on your guard."

"I don't need a lecture, thanks." She stomps harder and faster as she grows angrier. "You haven't had any interest in what I do for weeks now. There's no reason for you to pretend you care now."

I furrow my brow, caught off guard by her sharp words. Is that what she thinks? That I don't care? That couldn't be further from the truth. All I've ever done regarding Marie is because I care about her.

Her house isn't far from the bar, and we reach it a few

minutes later. She climbs the three short steps to her porch, and I hurry to catch up before she can go inside.

"I'm just looking out for you," I tell her, grabbing her hand to stop her from opening the door.

She jerks out of my grip as she whirls to face me. "I don't need you to look out for me! I'm not your responsibility."

I stare down at her, at a loss for words. Not my responsibility? I think of the promise I made Mom, and how hard I've been trying to keep it. How much I've had to fight to resist my desire for Marie. If I didn't feel so fucking responsible for her, we wouldn't be standing here, having this argument.

She'd be underneath me, naked and moaning in pleasure as I drive my cock into her again and again.

I clench my jaw and curl my hands into fists at my sides as frustration burns through me. I've been trying so hard to do what I thought was the right thing, but it's only made her resent me. Despite my best intentions, I only ever seem to screw things up with her.

"Look, I can take care of myself," she grumbles, waving her hand dismissively. "I don't need you looking out for me."

Now that pisses me off. It's hard to say why, but hearing her say that she doesn't need me makes me want to prove her wrong. She needs me... even if she doesn't want to admit it. She needs me the same way I need her. I know how badly she wants me. There's no way her desire has died off so quickly, and if she won't let me protect her, then I'll make damn sure I take care of her in other ways.

Closing the gap between us, I grab her waist and yank her against me. Her eyes go wide and she gasps, but I drop my lips to hers and kiss her before she can say a word. The kiss is hard and desperate. I press her up against her door and cup her face in one hand while my other keeps a firm hold of her waist. She grabs the front of my shirt and I expect her to push me away, but instead, she curls her fingers into the fabric and clings to me.

Our tongues tangle and I'm lost to the feel of her against me and the taste of her lips. Fuck, I missed this. I can't deny it. She just feels so damn good... so right. This feels so natural and easy, especially compared to the effort it takes me to resist her. When I kiss her, nothing else seems to matter. It all fades into the background, and there's only me and her.

I want more. I want to feel her soft skin against mine again. I want her body wrapped around mine as she moans and whimpers in my ear.

Glancing around to make sure there's no one out on the street, I move the hand I have on her waist down to the skirt of her short dress, I grab it and yank it up so I can reach between her legs and touch her. When I drag my finger along her panties, she hisses in a breath and I growl. She's already wet... her panties damp.

"Fuck, Marie," I murmur against her lips. "You want me bad, don't you?"

"Yeah," she breathes, not bothering to lie or play hard to get. "But you want me too."

She reaches down and cups the growing bulge in the front of my pants. I grunt and grind myself against her palm, at the end of my control. Reaching around her, I grab hold of her doorknob. It's time we took this inside...

Marie shoves me back and ducks under my arm, her hand covering her mouth. She rushes to the edge of her porch and leans over the railing. The next second, she starts vomiting into the bushes in front of the house.

Rushing to her side, I pull her hair back from her face to keep it out of her way. She continues to be sick for several moments until she's dry heaving. Finally, she's able to stop and leans against the railing as she catches her breath. Unsure what else to do, I rub her back and continue to keep her hair out of her face.

"Are you okay?" I ask gently.

Panting, she straightens and looks up at me. Her face is pale and her eyelids half-closed.

"I'm fine," she whispers. "I... I think I just want to go to bed."

"All right, I'll help you."

She tries to protest. "No, it's okay..."

"You're not getting rid of me that easily," I tell her, looping my arm around her waist. "You need help. I didn't realize you were so drunk, so let me help you get inside and up to bed, okay?"

"I'm not drunk," she mumbles, but I ignore that as I help her get to the front door.

Opening it, I take her inside and we make our way upstairs to her bedroom. I only let her go when we're inside the room and I'm certain she won't fall down the stairs or stumble and hurt herself. She goes into her bathroom and shuts the door. The water turns on in her sink. As I wait for her to come back out, I can't help but wonder how I didn't notice that she was so drunk to the point of getting sick. She seemed perfectly coherent the entire time we've been together. She doesn't even smell like alcohol.

What does that mean for our fight? Did she only say those things because she's intoxicated? They'd seemed so sincere—her anger so real.

It's possible being drunk only made her more honest. Whatever the case may be, it's not something I should worry about right now. I just need to make sure that she's okay and get her settled for the night.

A few minutes later, Marie opens the bathroom door and steps out. She's changed into an oversized t-shirt that barely reaches her thighs, so when she walks, I get a good look at her panties. My cock twitches at the sight, and I struggle to keep my lust under control. Now's not the time. Hold your shit together, man!

Marie drags her feet to her bed and climbs up and buries herself under the covers. I move to the side of the bed and sit next to her. With a gentle touch, I brush her hair back from her forehead.

"Do you want to get you some water?" I ask.

"I'm okay," she murmurs. Her eyes are already closed. "I swear, I'm not drunk."

Sure she's not. I'm not going to argue with her, though. She doesn't have a fever, so I doubt she's sick because she's got a bug. It doesn't really matter. I don't care if she's drunk. I've been worse than her plenty of times before. She's in bed now, safe and sound, and that's all I really care about.

"All right," I say in a soft voice. "Get some sleep and I'll check in with you in the morning, okay?"

"M'kay," she mumbles, snuggling deeper into her blankets.

I lean down and press a soft kiss at her temple. She's kind of adorable like this. I sit a few more minutes until her breathing grows even and steady. She's fast asleep.

Slowly and carefully, I make my way to the bedroom door. I pause to look back at her and my heart twists in my chest at how peaceful she looks. A part of me wants to go back, climb into bed next to her, and hold her until morning.

I resist the urge, telling myself that she's sick. She might wake up and not even remember what all happened tonight. Releasing a long breath, I turn and continue down the hallway, down the stairs, and out the front door, making sure to lock it before I close it behind me. When I reach the sidewalk, I turn back to gaze up at her house.

My lips still tingle from our kiss. What am I going to do? I'm not sure if I can continue with this back and forth with Marie for much longer. Every time I think I have myself under control with her, something happens and my desire wins. I just can't seem to stop myself. Do I just stop fighting it? Give in and pursue whatever it is I'm feeling for her?

Where would that leave me with my promise to Mom? The thought of her being disappointed in me for not taking care of Marie like a sister is something I can't stand.

Shaking my head, I walk away from the house. One way or another, I have to figure this out, because if I don't, I'm only going to end up hurting Marie even more than I already have. That's not what Mom would want either.

It's time for me to grow some balls and make my choice.

CHAPTER SEVENTEEN
MARIE

My stomach is killing me. I was hoping a good night's sleep would make me feel better, but I'm nauseous and have a dull headache throbbing behind my eyes. Curling up under my blankets, I debate whether to even get out of bed. What's wrong with me? I haven't been feeling great the last few days, and I thought it was due to stress and my confused emotions about Garrett.

Now I'm not so sure. This feels like something more. Like I'm actually sick.

God, last night was such a mess. The creep on the dance floor. Garrett coming to my rescue and walking me home. Our kiss.

That kiss! It was so hot, and then I ruined it when I threw up. Garrett was so gentle and caring as he took care of me afterward. Of course, he assumed I was drunk, which I wasn't—I didn't drink a drop of alcohol last night. I was just too exhausted to argue with him, and fell asleep before he left.

I think he kissed my forehead. He brushed the hair from my face, his fingertips light along my skin. Soothing. Comforting. It felt really good to have someone taking care of me like that.

Too bad I still feel like total shit.

Groaning, I roll over and reach for my phone on my side table. Garrett said he was going to check in on me this morning, and indeed, I have a missed call. It's not from Garrett, but Haven. What could she want at seven in the morning?

Bringing up her number, I hit dial, and she answers after just a few rings.

"Hey you," she says. "I heard from Maggie you guys went out last night. I wanted to make sure you were okay."

I close my eyes and hold back a groan. Maggie must have told her we ran into Garrett.

"I'm good," I tell her, my voice raspy, making it very clear that I'm not, in fact, good.

"Woah, are you sure?" Haven's tone takes on genuine concern. "You sound kind of rough."

"It's nothing. I've just been dealing with a stomach issue. No big deal."

"Do you need anything?" she asks. "It's Saturday, so no daycare. I can come over and bring you Pepto or something."

"I appreciate the offer, but I promise, I'll be fine." I don't want her to worry about me and make a fuss. "It's just a stomach ache. I have to work today anyway, so I can grab some Pepto myself if I need it while I'm out."

"Well, at least you're not pregnant or anything," Haven says with a teasing chuckle. "I can tell you that nausea is something else. It knocked me on my ass for days at a time."

My heart comes to a sudden stop. Pregnant?

"Right," I mumble, forcing a laugh, even though I am not feeling any bit of amusement. "That would be crazy."

"Let me know if you need anything, okay?" she insists. "I'll come over right away."

"Okay, I will."

Hanging up the call, I sit up and drop my phone on the bed

next to me. Pressing my back against the headboard, I stare straight ahead, dumbfounded. Pregnant? Could I be pregnant?

No, we used a condom. I remember him getting it and putting it on. He got it out of his wallet...wait! That's bad for condoms, right? You're not supposed to keep them in a wallet. Did it break? I didn't see when he took it off and threw it away... would he have noticed if it broke? What if I am pregnant? I can only imagine how Garrett would react. Would he think I got knocked up on purpose to trap him or something?

As if my thoughts have somehow manifested him, my phone buzzes and Garrett's name pops up. He's just sent a text.

Hesitantly, I open it.

Garrett: Hey, hope you're feeling okay this morning. Let me know if you need anything. I'm sorry about last night.

Another apology? Is it for the kiss? That only makes me feel even shittier. He's apologizing for that hot-as-hell kiss, and I might be incubating his oops-baby right now.

I quickly type a response.

Marie: I'm okay. Thanks for getting me home.

I don't know what else to say to him right now. Do I tell him I suspect I could be pregnant? No, no... I shouldn't do that. There's a good chance that I'm not, and I'd just be dropping a bombshell for no reason. It'd be better to figure out if I am preg nant before I say anything to him... if I say anything to him. Wait, of course I'd tell him if I was pregnant! Wouldn't I? Yes, he would deserve to know... but I'm probably not pregnant, so I'm getting worked up for no reason.

But if I am pregnant...

Shit, I'm spiraling. I need to calm down and think logically.

Releasing a long, steadying breath, I decide that a trip to the pharmacy over my lunch break is what I need. I'll grab a pregnancy test. Once I know for sure one way or another if I'm pregnant, I'll figure out my next step.

I just have to make it until lunch so I can take the test, and when it's negative, I'll pretend this never happened.

"MARIE, are you okay? You seem distracted again today."

Blinking, I look over at Kathy, who's frowning at me in concern. Shit, I was spacing out again. I just can't focus on work today. If I keep this up, Kathy's going to fire me for being totally useless. My nerves are too wired to concentrate on anything except for what could possibly be going on inside me. Time seems to crawl as I wait for my lunch break so I can finally get that test.

"I'm fine," I assure her, nearly choking on the lie. "Just feeling under the weather, that's all."

"Oh, dear! Do you need to go home? I'd hate for you to feel like you have to work if you're not feeling well."

I give her a small smile. She's such a sweet, understanding person. Not all bosses would be as concerned about me as she is.

"I appreciate that, Kathy, but I'm going to run to the pharmacy at lunch and pick up... medicine. I'll be all right after that."

"If you're sure." Kathy checks her watch and then looks around the library. There aren't many people visiting today. "Why don't you go ahead and take an early lunch? I've got things under control here."

"Really?" My heart leaps and I have to fight to keep the eagerness out of my voice. "That'd be great, Kathy. Thank you."

"No problem, dear."

I gather my keys and purse and make my way out of the library. The drive to the pharmacy feels like it takes forever, but it's only about five minutes away. Parking outside of the store, I take a few minutes to catch my breath and build up my courage to go inside. God, please don't run into anyone I know in there.

Finally, I force myself to get out of the car and walk through the sliding doors into the pharmacy. I make a beeline for the pregnancy tests, keeping my head ducked, praying no one notices me. Grabbing three boxes of the first brand I find, I hurry to the cash register, pay for the test, and practically run out the door and back to my car.

Holy shit! That was way more nerve wracking than I expected. My stomach is rolling and I think I'm going to be sick again.

No way can I go back to work. I'm feeling even worse than I did this morning, and if the test is positive...

Fuck! I grab my phone and dial the library's number.

"Blue Ridge Falls Public Library, how can I help you?" Kathy answers.

"Hey, Kathy. It's Marie. I'm feeling even worse than before, so I think I'm going to take the rest of the day off if that's all right?"

"Of course!" she replies. "It's not a problem. You just focus on feeling better."

"Thanks, Kathy."

Once we hang up, I start the car and make the drive home. When I get there, I grab the test and hurry inside and up the stairs to my bathroom.

I open the test and sit on the toilet and... nothing.

Oh, God, I'm so nervous I can't pee!

Shit, shit, shit. I turn on the sink and let the water run.

Think wet thoughts... streams... ocean waves... come on! Pee!

At last, I'm able to take the test, and then it's just more waiting. I leave the test on the counter by the sink and pace the small room as I count down the three minutes until the results appear.

It's all going to be okay. Realistically, what are the chances of me being pregnant? I think an average woman in her twenties has like 25% of getting pregnant every month, so really, what are the odds?

No amount of rationalization is helping my nerves, though. I continue to pace and start chewing at my fingernails in agitation. Finally, the timer on my phone goes off and I dive for the test. It takes me a few moments to comprehend what I'm seeing.

Two pink lines.

Oh, fuck.

They're pretty faint, though. Maybe it's a false positive?

I grab for the other tests and take a second one...and then the third.

I get two pink lines each time.

Slowly, I sink down to the bathroom floor, the tests clutched between my hands. I can't tear my gaze away from those lines. Positive. It's positive.

I'm fucking pregnant.

A whirlwind of emotions overwhelms me. Shock, fear, uncertainty... but also, strangely, a flicker of excitement.

I'm going to have a baby. I'm going to be a mommy.

My heart hammers in my chest as I drop one hand to my belly. There's a little being inside me right now. It's so tiny, but it's mine. Mine... and Garrett's.

Garrett. How in the world am I going to tell Garrett? Things are so complicated right now, and I have no idea how he'll react. I'm terrified that he's going to be upset. He's made it abundantly clear that he doesn't want to be with me, and now this... what will he think of me?

I rub my hand over my belly and murmur, "Don't you

worry, baby. I'm going to figure this out. Whatever happens, it's not your fault. I don't want you to think for one second that you aren't loved."

Is it silly for me to be talking to it already? Maybe, but it's also oddly comforting. Suddenly, I'm not alone. I'm going to matter to someone who loves me. I won't just be an obligation or a burden to my kid. They'll need me and want me around because it's me... their mom.

My heart swells at the thought and I hug myself, tight.

I'm going to do whatever I have to in order to protect my baby. I won't treat my child the way my Dad has been treating me lately. They'll be cared for and loved, and will never question whether they're wanted. Even if Garrett doesn't feel the same way, this baby will never doubt its place with me.

Pushing to my feet, I set the pregnancy test back on the counter and wash my hands. As I dry them, I gaze at myself in the mirror. I look pale and tired, with bags under my eyes. Really, I look like shit, and I still feel like crap, but that's not my biggest concern anymore.

I'm not sure what I'm going to do, so maybe it's for the best that I don't tell Garrett about the pregnancy yet. I'll keep it a secret from him for the time being while I figure out what to do and how to tell him. I should talk to Haven, though...she'll be able to help me.

Raising my chin, I give my reflection a confident once over. The next second, my stomach flips and the nausea hits me hard and fast.

Damn it!

I lunge for the toilet, throwing the seat up just in time. I empty the contents of my stomach into the porcelain bowl and moan in misery as I continue to keep my head draped over the edge. Well, at least I know why I'm sick... not that it makes me feel any less terrible.

Placing my hand back on my stomach, I mumble, "You better be cute as hell."

Then, I get sick again.

CHAPTER EIGHTEEN
GARRETT

Staring at my computer screen, I try to make sense of what I'm doing, but my brain feels like mush. I'm working on my final project for finance class; building a financial model for a hypothetical company. The project involves creating an Excel model with inputs, assumptions, and financial projections, mocking a sensitivity analysis to show how changes in assumptions impact outcomes, and ultimately, writing a report explaining the rationale behind the model's design.

This project has been a beast, sucking up all my time and attention. It's been over a week since I've been back to the library because I've been putting all my focus into this final. Marie wouldn't be able to help me with this anyway. It's my finance class, not the English class, and I'm supposed to work on it myself, using all the knowledge I've gained throughout the course. I'm just about done, which is a huge relief. Looking up from my laptop screen, I gaze around my kitchen and flinch at how much of a mess my place is. Dishes are piled in the sink, the trash needs taken out, laundry is scattered around the living room.

Groaning, I turn my attention back to the computer. I just

need to finish up the last of the report and submit it, and then I'm done.

And... send.

I slump back in my chair and let out a groan of relief. Thank God. It's over. I can finally breathe again.

Pushing to my feet, I stretch my neck side-to-side and raise my hands above my head to work the knots out of my shoulders. Looking around at the mess around me, I just feel exhausted. I need to get out of here. Get some fresh air and interact with people. It seems like it's been days since I've seen another person. I haven't even talked to Haven beyond a few proof-of-life text messages.

I get cleaned up, showering and changing my clothes before grabbing my keys and heading out the door. Deciding it's been a minute since I've seen my sister, I head out to her and Christian's acreage just outside of town. When I reach the property, I drive up the long, winding driveway to the huge two-story farmhouse and park in an open spot in front of the garage. I make my way up to the porch, and before I reach the door, it swings open and Haven appears in the doorway. She's wearing sweatpants and a sweatshirt, and has her long auburn hair piled into a messy bun on top of her head. Her brows raise in surprise as she looks me up and down.

"Garrett? What are you doing here?"

"Hey," I reply, grinning. "I just finished my final and thought I'd swing by and see how you're doing. Christian messaged me and let me know you were taking a few days off from work because you haven't been feeling well. Everything okay?"

She chuckles and rests a hand on her visibly pregnant belly. Five months in and she's looking plump and healthy. I never really bought into the whole pregnant-woman glow thing, but I can see it in Haven. There's something about her that just seems to be brighter.

"I'm fine," she says with a teasing grin. I notice a bit of tension in her eyes. She must be tired. "It was just a cold...that's the risk of working in a daycare, you know? I'm surrounded by human petri dishes. I'm feeling much better, though, and I'm happy to see you! It's been so long. We were about to send a search party. Congratulations on finishing your final! Come on inside."

She moves to let me into her large two-story farmhouse home and we make our way to the living room. There are toy trucks and blocks spread across the floor that we tiptoe through, and extra pillows and fuzzy blankets all over the couch. It almost looks like a nest that I assume Haven has been hunkering down in whenever she gets the chance.

"Take a seat," she says. "I just made a pot of tea. I'll get you a cup."

"Thanks." I settle on the couch as she disappears down the hallway toward the kitchen. A few minutes later, she returns holding two cups of steaming tea and hands one to me.

Once she's made herself comfortable in an armchair next to me, she lets out a little sigh and gives me a sleepy smile.

"You've finally finished your class," she says. "You must be so relieved."

I nod. "You have no idea."

"Good, good," she murmurs, "I'm proud of you."

I take a sip of my tea and she stares down into hers, seemingly lost in thought.

Frowning, I ask, "Hey, you okay?"

Blinking, she jerks her gaze back up to mine. "Huh? Oh, yeah. I'm fine."

"Are you sure? Seems like you've got something on your mind."

She shakes her head and says, "It's nothing, I'm good. Just, uh, tired. Pregnancy fatigue."

Concerned, I furrow my brow. "Is that unusual? Is everything okay with the baby?"

"Everything's fine," she assures me. "It's just hard work growing a human, you know?"

"Yeah, I suppose it is." I take another sip of my tea. There's another subject I want to bring up with her, but I don't know how to do so in a casual way that won't raise her suspicions. "So, uh, what did I miss while I was locked away? How's Christian and Oliver?"

"Christian's good," she says. "Busy with work, but since he's got an office in town now, he doesn't have to go to the city nearly so often. Oliver is a little fireball. He's excited for the new baby, but I also think he's feeling a little anxious. It's a big change, after all."

"Uh huh. I'm sure. And... Marie?"

To my surprise, Haven looks away from me and her expression becomes unreadable.

"Marie's good," she answers simply.

That's it? That's all I get? Have is usually more forthcoming than this. Why's she so tightlipped now? I thought Marie and I were good. Did something happen that I don't know about?

"Have you talked to her lately?" The question feels silly because the two talk to each other daily. Still, I want to see if I can dig out any morsel of info about Marie that I can.

"I have..." She slowly replies, but again, she doesn't expand on her answer. It's like she really doesn't want to talk to me about Marie at all.

"Okay," I murmur, feeling awkward as I take another drink of tea. I want to press the issue, but I also don't want to seem like I'm desperate and digging for information... even though that's exactly what I'm doing. Instead, I let the issue drop and change the subject instead.

"Getting ready for the baby?" I ask.

She immediately relaxes and her face lights up. "Yes! We actually just finished putting the nursery together. Do you want to see it?"

I grin, her enthusiasm infectious. "I'd love to."

Standing, I help Haven to her feet and she leads me out of the living room, up the stairs, and down the hall to a closed door with a little sign hanging on it. The sign has lambs and flowers and says 'Nursery' in rainbow letters.

"This is it," she says, pushing open the door.

The nursery is bright and cheerful, painted a soft, buttery yellow. There's a crib in the corner, a rocking chair by the window, and shelves already filled with stuffed animals and books. Sunlight streams in, highlighting the playful decals of clouds and stars that Haven must have painstakingly placed on the walls.

"It's perfect," I say, and I mean it. "You and Christian did a great job with this."

Haven beams, her hand instinctively going to her belly. "We wanted it to feel warm, you know? Like a little haven—pun absolutely intended—for the baby."

I chuckle, but my smile falters as my thoughts shift again. The joy radiating from her is genuine, and I'm happy for her, but there's something gnawing at me. Something—or rather someone—she refuses to talk about.

"It's going to be great," I say, stepping toward the crib and running a hand along the smooth wooden railing. "You're going to be a fantastic mom."

"Thanks, Garrett," she says softly, leaning against the rocking chair. "Being Oliver's stepmom has been wonderful, but

I have to admit, I'm nervous for there to be two kids in the house. I hope Christian and I can handle it."

"You'll be fine," I assure her.

She gives me a sad smile and confesses, "I... I really wish Mom were here to give me advice and tell me everything's going to be okay. I miss her so much."

Tears slip out of her eyes and down her cheeks. I cross the room to wrap my arms around her in a tight hug.

"I know," I say against her hair. "I miss her too. She'd be so proud of you, Haven, and I'm sure she'd tell you just how great of a job you're doing as a mom."

Haven buries her face against my chest and we stand like that for a while, seeking comfort from each other as we both feel the sting of our loss. At length, I gently pull back and smile down at her. Cupping her face, I brush away her tears with my thumbs.

"No more crying," I tell her. "Mom would want you to enjoy this time. She'd want us both to be happy, right?"

She swallows and nods. "You're right."

I kiss her forehead. "I should get going and you should get some rest, okay? I'll check in with you later."

She releases a small sigh. "Okay. Thanks, Garrett. It's hard to talk about Mom, even with Christian. Being able to admit how much I miss her is... soothing. You know?"

"Yeah, I get it." My heart twists and I step back before turning for the door. "If you ever need to, you know you can always talk to me. I'm here for you, no matter what."

"I know, Garrett." She waves at me as I head out the door. "See you later."

I make my way downstairs and through the hallway to the front door. As I'm passing a side table pressed up against the wall, I notice a gift bag decorated in pastel flowers and zoo animals. I pause, glancing over my shoulder to make sure Haven hasn't come down the stairs to catch me peeking. Finding the gift tag, I turn it over. Marie's name is written in black across the small white square. Carefully, I reach into the bag and pull aside the yellow tissue paper. I find a copy of the book *What to Expect When You're Expecting* inside. Thoughtful gift. Marie *would* give Haven and Christian a book as a baby present.

I stare down at her name for a few moments longer, my chest aching and my stomach twisting with longing. Why didn't Haven seem to want to talk about Marie? What's going on there?

Sighing, I drop the gift tag back into the bag and continue onto the front door. Damn it... I miss her. A part of me wants to reach out to her and see how things are, but I'm admittedly nervous. I haven't spoken to her since the night I walked her home from the bar and we kissed. I texted her the next day to make sure she was okay. She said she was, but that was it. Is she upset about the kiss? Does she even remember it?

Once I'm outside, I head for my truck. I should talk to Marie, but I can't screw it up again, so I want to make sure I'm prepared before seeing her. I need to apologize properly and try to repair what I can of our friendship. Things won't be the same, I know that, but I don't want to lose her even if we can't be together the way she wants. I'm supposed to have a PT appointment tomorrow afternoon. Maybe I'll stop by the library afterward and see how she's doing. That should give me plenty of time to come up with the right thing to say... whatever that might be.

Feeling more at ease now that I have a plan, I climb into my truck and take off down the driveway, feeling somewhat lighter.

For the first time since before my accident, it feels like things are finally falling into place for me. Everything is going right, and I'm going to do all that I can to make sure it stays that way.

CHAPTER NINETEEN
MARIE

The nausea just won't let up. Waking up in the morning has become a kind of torture because I just feel like shit, and it seems to get worse every day. I can hardly keep food or water down, and I've missed more work in the last week than the entire time I've been with the library. Meredith has also been getting frustrated with me since I keep telling her I can't help with the kids and has been pushing me for a reason why I'm so sick - because it's such an inconvenience for her - so I've been dodging her calls the last couple days.

Morning sickness shouldn't be this bad. Is something wrong with me?

Ugh, I don't want to get out of bed, but missing another day of work is out of the question. Leaving poor Kathy in the lurch so often lately makes me feel guilty, so I force myself to get up and get ready for the day.

I shower, dress, and try to eat something, but I can barely force down a piece of toast. By the time I'm ready to leave for work, my body's exhausted, but I push through. I can do this. Staying at home and feeling sorry for myself isn't going to make me feel any better. Getting back into my regular routine and adjusting to this pregnancy will help me feel better.

By the time I arrive at the library, I'm wishing I'd just stayed home. My stomach is rolling and I've almost thrown up about five times. When I walk into the library and get to the front desk, Kathy looks up at me, and then frowns in concern.

"Marie? Are you feeling better?"

"I'm feeling all right."

"Are you sure?" She looks far from convinced. "If you need another day…"

I quickly shake my head. "No, no, I've missed enough work. I'm fine, really. I want to be here, and I want to work."

"If you're sure," she sighs, though she still appears cautious.

"Absolutely." I set my purse down at my desk and do my best not to appear weak and tired. The morning crawls by after that. I do my best to ignore my upset stomach, and eventually, it calms down to a manageable dull ache.

Near noon, I notice a stack of books sitting on the counter behind the front desk and move to grab them.

"You don't have to worry about those," Kathy insists when she sees me picking up the stack. "I can put them away."

A quick scan of the titles causes me to shake my head. "These go on the top shelf in the mystery section, Kathy. You know you shouldn't be climbing up on the step stool."

"I don't think you should be doing so either." She gives me a concerned look. "You look really pale. If you're this sick, you should go home and rest."

Waving my hand to dismiss her concern, I insist, "My stomach aches, but my legs are just fine. I can put these books away, no problem. I'll be right back."

"Marie, hold on…"

I'm already walking away, grabbing the step stool, moving from around the desk and heading toward the mystery section.

It's a few rows in, but when I reach it, I spot the open slots on the shelf above where the books should go. Unfolding the stool, I climb onto it, holding my stack in one arm. Grabbing the book at the top of the pile, I reach to put where it belongs... and I'm struck by a sudden wave of dizziness.

My stomach pitches and I sway on my feet as everything goes blurry. Confused and panicked, I drop the books and reach out to try and grab hold of the shelves to steady myself, but my hands slip. The next moment, my foot slips on the stool and I fall. Time seems to slow, and I'm suspended midair, staring up at the blurry ceiling in shock. I don't have time to really feel fear or worry. This is bad and going to hurt. Still, I don't even yell out... I'm too stunned.

Time rushes back to normal, and I hit the floor, hard. That's when I release a cry as pain ripples through me and stars explode in my vision. Before I can fully comprehend just how bad this could really be for me—for my baby—darkness creeps in and then everything goes black.

PAIN IS the first thing I become conscious of. My back hurts, my head throbs, and my tailbone is sore. Groaning, my eyes blink open at the bright lights above me. God, what happened? Where am I?

"Marie? Are you awake?"

Haven sits beside me. Her brow is furrowed with concern, and she's holding my hand. I become aware of a steady beeping and then the IV in my arm. Wait... am I in the hospital?

Frowning, I look around and realize that I am indeed in a hospital room, lying in a hospital bed.

"What... what happened?" I murmur. My mouth is dry and my throat is sore, so my voice comes out raspy.

Haven squeezes my hand. "You collapsed. Kathy heard you fall and found you unconscious among the bookshelves. She called 911, and an ambulance brought you here."

Oh, shit. I collapsed. I remember the dizziness and losing my footing. Falling to the floor.

"The baby? Is the baby okay?"

Haven nods and assures me, "Yes, don't worry about the baby. It's completely fine."

Thank God! I sag against my pillows in relief and gaze up at Haven, who's staring down at me with a mixture of worry and relief in her gaze. After finding out I was pregnant, I went to Haven. She's the only one who knows. I also confessed to her that Garrett is the father, and though she was initially shocked, I made her promise not to say anything to him. She agreed, but I had to promise her to tell him, eventually.

"How are you feeling?" Haven asks. "Are you in a lot of pain?"

I shrug, which makes me groan. "It could be worse. I'll definitely be sore for a few days. Did the doctor say if anything was broken?"

"No, there's nothing like that," she tells me. "You'll be bruised for a while, and it might not be super comfortable to sit for a couple days, but that's the worst of it. The doctor seemed more concerned about why you collapsed."

"Did they say why?"

She shakes her head. "They ran some tests while you were out and the doctor should be back at any moment with the results."

As if on cue, there's a knock on the door.

"Come in!" Haven calls out.

The door swings open and in strolls a tall, older man with a head of thick silver hair and black square glasses perched on his nose. He comes to a stop next to my bed and I squint so I can read his nametag.

Dr. Taylor.

"Glad to see you awake, Marie," he says with a smile as he looks me over. "How are you feeling?"

"Sore. Can you tell me what happened, doctor? Why did I collapse?"

"You're severely dehydrated due to hyperemesis gravidarum," he explains. "It's a condition where you have severe morning sickness that lasts longer and is more debilitating than normal. I'm guessing you haven't been able to keep a lot of food and fluids down?"

"Everything makes me want to vomit. I try to eat and drink, but it just makes the nausea worse."

He nods. "I thought as much. We're pumping you with fluids through your IV, so that will help your dehydration. I want you to stay here for a day or two so we can monitor you and make sure you're able to retain some sustenance before we let you go, okay?"

"Okay," I say, my heart sinking. The last thing I want is to be held up in the hospital, but I know I have to be careful. It's not just about me anymore. I have to think of what's best for the baby.

The doctor talks for a little longer, but I can't really understand everything he says. I'm too tired and the throbbing in the back of my head is insistent on stealing my attention. Thankfully, Haven stays the whole time and appears to hang onto Dr. Taylor's every word.

"I'll be back to check on you later, Marie," the doctor finally says. "You just rest and try to eat something if you can, all right?"

"I'll try," I assure him.

"Good." He grins. "I'll see you later."

He leaves the room and Haven and I are silent as we wait for the doors to click shut behind him.

Turning back to me, Haven asks, "Do you think we should call Garrett and tell him you're here?"

My heart seizes at the thought, though I know she's just being reasonable. Garrett still doesn't know anything about my pregnancy. Haven has been true to her word and hasn't made a peep about it to him, which I know hasn't been easy for her. She and Garrett share just about everything, and I feel guilty asking her to keep such a colossal secret from him.

However, I'm so angry with him still that I don't even want to think about seeing him right now. He keeps disappearing on me, and I'm getting sick of it. He doesn't want to talk to me for a week? Fine...I can handle this by myself.

Shaking my head, I reply, "No, no, I don't want him to find out like this."

She frowns. "When do you plan on telling him, then?"

"I... I don't know. Soon."

"Soon?"

"Yes, I promise, I'll tell him, but I don't want to tell him like this. Not when I'm feeling like crap and falling off of stools. It'll only make him more upset."

Haven hesitates, and I can tell she's wrestling with this. I feel like such a bad friend for asking her to keep this secret for me. It's shitty and selfish, and she hates lying to Garrett by omission. I just don't know what to do. I can't stand the thought of him getting angry with me, or feeling as though he's obligated to be with me or something because of the baby. He'll be a good father and he'll love this child, but I don't know what he'll feel toward me. Frustration? Resentment?

If he hated me for this, I wouldn't be able to stand it.

At length, Haven sighs. "Okay, okay, I understand. I

promised I wouldn't say anything to him, but you have to know you can't keep this from him forever."

"I know," I say. "I just need some time, but I will tell him. I swear."

Giving me a small smile, Haven squeezes my hand again. I gaze up at her, grateful for her presence and for her support. At the same time, I can't help feeling a little envious of her. She's pregnant with the man she loves, and the two of them couldn't be more thrilled. I'm pregnant with the man I love, and I'm dreading even telling him...because I don't know if he loves me back. I'm going to have to. I know I will. Especially now that I've been so sick.

Blue Ridge Falls is a small town, and I've no doubt rumors will spread about why I'm in the hospital. Those rumors will reach my family, and I can already hear my dad's lecture about being irresponsible and not thinking about the consequences of my actions. However, those rumors are also going to reach Garrett... I just hope he doesn't grow suspicious.

He needs to hear this from me before anyone else, so I need to somehow find the courage to rip the bandaid off and tell him.

My stomach twists with nausea again, but this time, it's not because of my morning sickness. It's from the fear that I might push the only man I've ever loved away with the truth, but I have to tell him and take that risk whether I like it or not.

CHAPTER TWENTY
GARRETT

Pulling up to the hospital, I park my truck and release a long breath. I can't wait until I don't have to come here anymore. This is one of my last physical therapy sessions. Part of me doesn't really think I need to anymore; I feel great and am ready to finally put the accident fully behind him. At the same time, I don't want to do anything to mess up my recovery, so I get out of my truck and trudge up to the hospital's entrance.

Check in is fast and I make my way toward the PT offices. On the way, I pass by the closed door to the maternity ward. A familiar figure suddenly turns the corner ahead of me and I come to an immediate stop. Haven is walking slowly, her head ducked as she looks through some sort of pamphlet in her hand.

"Haven?"

She looks up, startled, and comes to an immediate stop.

"Garrett? What are you doing here?" she asks, looking more anxious than happy to see me, which puts me instantly on alert. Something's wrong.

"I'm here for physical therapy," I explain cautiously. "What are you doing here? Do you have an appointment?"

Why isn't Christian here with her?

She blinks and seems to take a moment to comprehend what I've just asked.

"Oh... oh, yeah! Yeah, that's why I'm here. Just a regular check-up. That's all."

I arch a brow. I'm definitely not buying that. She's visibly nervous, her leg bouncing up and down, and she keeps glancing around as if afraid someone's going to spot us here together.

"Haven, what the hell...?"

Before I can finish my sentence, a nurse appears at my side and looks between me and Haven.

"Excuse me, I didn't mean to interrupt," she says before focusing solely on Haven. "I knew you went down to the cafeteria, so I just wanted to let you know that they've finished Marie's exam if you want to go back to her room."

Haven's face drains of color as she says, "Great... thank you."

The nurse turns and hurries away, leaving Haven and I alone again. I stare down at my sister, confused and stunned.

"Haven... why is Marie here? Why is she in the maternity ward? What's going on?"

Haven swallows and fidgets with her pamphlet, which I can see is about something called hyperemesis gravidarum. Her eyes go wide with anxiety.

"Garrett, look... there's a good explanation for all this..."

"Haven," I say in a firmer voice. "Don't try to give me any bullshit excuses. I can tell when you're lying. What's wrong with Marie?"

She stares at me, and I can practically see her internal struggle playing out in her gaze. I don't break eye contact with her, not willing to give her an inch right now.

Finally, she releases a long sigh and her shoulder slump, as if in defeat.

"Marie... Marie is pregnant."

Everything around me seems to slow to a crawl. Pregnant? No... no, that can't be right. Marie can't be pregnant. If she's pregnant, then that would mean I'm...

"Where is she?"

"Garrett, you need to take a beat here," Haven says. "I know you're upset..."

"Haven, for God sakes, take me to Marie, now!"

She closes her eyes and takes a deep breath.

"All right," she replies at length. "Come with me."

She turns and leads me through the doors to the maternity ward. We make our way down the corridor until we reach a half open door and she pauses to look back at me.

"Just... be gentle with her, okay?"

I don't say anything as she pushes the door all the way open and we walk inside. When I cross the threshold into the room, I freeze at the sight of Marie lying in the hospital bed. She's hooked up to an IV and heart monitor. She looks pale, her brown hair spread out on her pillow. Weak. Like the life was literally being drained out of her.

Marie turns her head when Haven and I walk into the room, and when her dark eyes land on me, they go wide and she struggles to sit up.

"Wha-what are you doing here?" she gasps, looking around frantically, as if searching for an escape.

I cross to her bed and gaze down at her, my brow furrowed.

"Marie, why didn't you tell me you were pregnant?"

She freezes and visibly tenses, her shoulders going rigid, and her fingers curling into her blankets. Clearing her throat, she looks up at me, attempting to appear nonchalant as she shrugs.

"Why do you assume it's yours?"

That pisses me right the fuck off. I narrow my eyes at her.

"Don't bullshit me, Marie," I growl. "We both know I'm the only one you've been with lately, just like you're the only one

I've been with. I wouldn't lie to you about that and I know you wouldn't either."

She looks irritated, dropping her gaze as her cheeks turn a light pink, not the same vibrant color as usual, though. She fidgets with her blanket.

"Fine," she murmurs. "There hasn't been anyone else but you."

My temper dissipates at her softly spoken confession, and I place a finger under her chin to tilt her face back up to mine.

"Marie, why are you in the hospital? Is something wrong with the baby?"

My heart twists at the thought, but I maintain a calm demeanor as I wait for her to respond. She releases a long sigh, slipping her chin from me.

"I've been having debilitating morning sickness," she confesses. "I'm exhausted and dehydrated. The baby is fine."

A mixture of relief and concern floods through me. I lay my hand on her forehead. Haven frowns at me.

"What are you doing?" she asks, while Marie stares up at me in confusion.

"I'm, uh... checking her temperature," I say, quickly dropping my hand. "That's what Mom always did when we were sick. Sorry."

Marie jerks her eyes from mine again. "The doctor has been keeping track of all that. Don't worry."

I nod, but I hate feeling useless, and I don't know how to help her right now.

"How long have you known?" I ask, my eyes dipping to her flat belly, hidden under the blankets.

"A couple weeks," she confesses.

Whirling on Haven, I say, "And you knew this? You've known all this time?"

She shrugs, looking unapologetic. "Pretty much, yes. I

promised to keep it a secret, and if you weren't such a brute, I wouldn't have spilled the beans. If you're expecting me to be sorry for holding onto the secret for as long as I did, I'm not, so take that scowl off your face right now. You look like Mom when she'd get angry."

"You're so annoying sometimes," I grumble before turning my attention back to Marie.

"Go easy on her," Marie says. "She was only doing what I asked her to do. Besides, it wasn't like you were around."

I flinch at her cool tone and bitter words. She's right. I disappeared on her again, running from her when I should've just talked to her like a fucking adult.

"Look, Marie...I'm sorry." I run a hand through my hair, taking a deep breath. "I can understand that you've been pissed at me and have been keeping this to yourself, but I know now.. No more secrets, okay? At least when it comes to the baby."

Marie hesitates before nodding. "Okay. No more secrets."

A tense, awkward silence falls between us. Marie looks at a loss for words, and I don't really know what to say either. This is all so overwhelming. Not only did I get a woman pregnant, but I got Marie pregnant. I'm supposed to take care of her, but instead, I've gotten her into a huge mess and thrown her life into chaos.

Fuck, how disappointed would Mom be in me right now? She would tell me I have to do the right thing. The responsible thing. I put Marie into this situation, and I'm not going to make her go through it alone.

"Um, what are you planning to do when you get out of the hospital?" I ask.

Marie shrugs. "Go home. Go to work. Basically, go back to normal."

"Normal isn't an option right now," I declare. "I'm going to help take care of you and you're going to take it easy until you are feeling better."

"Garrett!" Haven exclaims. "You can't just come in here and go all caveman on her like that."

Marie's jaw drops, and she shakes her head. "No, that's not necessary, Garrett. I'm already feeling a lot better since they've given me some fluids. I'll be fine."

I have no doubt that she's perfectly capable of taking care of herself. She's been doing so for a long time, on top of taking care of everyone else—her demanding father and stepmother, and stepping up to look after her siblings even when she should be focusing on herself. Things are different now. She's pregnant... with *my* baby.

"I need to take responsibility for all this. For you, and for the baby. Besides, you helped me when I needed it. Now I'm returning the favor... sort of."

That sounds too transactional, given that I'm the father of her child. Still, I'm not sure how else to approach this situation.

Marie gazes up at me with an expression that's difficult to read and Haven lets out a low growl next to me.

"Garrett, you are so stupid," my sister grumbles.

I shoot her a frown, confused. Before I can question her, Marie sighs.

"Is that the only reason you want to be involved?" she asks me softly. "Because you feel responsible? Obligated to do so?"

Looking between the two women, it's clear I've made a mistake, but I don't know what it is. I'm doing the right thing, aren't I? Stepping up so Marie isn't doing this by herself?

How am I the bad guy right now?

"I... I mean, yeah." I shrug. "What other reasons would there be?"

"My God," Haven groans, throwing up her hands and turning to walk right out of the room.

I watch her leave and turn back to Marie with a frown.

"What? What did I say?"

"It's nothing," she says under her breath. "Nevermind."

Lying back down, she rolls onto her side so her back is to me and doesn't say another word.

CHAPTER TWENTY-ONE

MARIE

Stepping outside for the first time in two days, I let the sun warm my face. I suck in a deep breath of fresh air and savor the fact that I don't feel like I'm going to throw up. My doctor told me I might continue to experience strong nausea for a while yet, but that it should pass before too long.

"Marie, are you ready to go home?"

Garrett walks up to me. His truck is parked by the curb behind him. Seeing his concerned but determined expression makes my chest ache. God, why does he insist on doing this? Caring for me and helping me through the pregnancy? I know he feels obligated, and most women would be thrilled to have the man who got them pregnant step up and take responsibility, but I don't feel good about this. I'm just another burden for him. Another mess he has to clean up.

That's the last thing I want.

Swallowing, I slowly nod. "Yeah... yeah, I'm ready."

He offers me his hand. I frown down at it before reluctantly taking it, too tired to argue. I just want to get home and burrow myself under my bedcovers and go to sleep.

Garrett helps me to his truck and up into the passenger seat.

He's treating me like I'm delicate and breakable. Not long ago, I'd have loved to receive this attention from him, but today, it just makes me want to curl up into a ball and cry. None of this would be happening if he didn't feel as though he had to do it.

He climbs in next to me and pulls away from the hospital. We don't speak for several minutes, but eventually, he clears his throat.

"I'm going to be at your beck and call from now on," he tells me matter-of-factly. "Day or night, don't hesitate to reach out to me if you need anything, okay? I don't want you to have to worry or stress about anything."

I rest my head against the cool glass of my window and gaze out at the passing houses.

"Okay."

"I'm serious, Marie," he says. "If you need groceries, a ride to work, anything, you let me know. I'd also like to be present for future appointments for the baby, if that's okay with you."

"Yeah... that's fine."

My emotions are tumultuous. I just want to go numb, so I don't have to feel anything right now.

"I want to be as involved as you'll allow me to be," Garrett continues. "You don't have to do any of this alone."

"Thank you, Garrett." I try to sound grateful, but my voice is too soft and my tone too sad. Does he notice? If he does, he doesn't say anything.

I should be grateful, relieved that he's so willing to be with me every step of the way with this, but he's not doing any of this because he feels real affection for me. He's doing it because he thinks it's the right thing to do.

He's being the good guy right now, but I wish he would just... I don't know. Not act like he cares about me when he really only cares about my pregnancy.

We soon arrive at my house and Garrett escorts me inside,

holding me up like he's afraid I'll tip over. He doesn't let me go until I'm settled on the couch. Grabbing a pillow, he puts it behind my head and drapes a blanket over my lap.

"Garrett, you don't have to do all this. I'll be fine, really."

"Just rest. I'll make you something to eat. Nothing too heavy, so it won't upset your stomach."

Before I can say anything, he turns and makes his way out of the living room and into the kitchen, moving pots and pans around. Sighing, I sink back into my pillow and pull the blanket up to cover my whole body. I'm so tired and heartsick. I just want to be cozy and forget about everything I've been through in the last few days.

Except I can't forget. I'll never be able to forget because the reminder is growing inside me right now.

Laying my hands on my belly, I murmur, "Oh, little bean. What kind of a mess am I bringing you into, hm? Your mommy is desperately in love with your daddy, but he just wants to be friends. Such a bummer, huh?"

Damn, I'm already complaining to my kid about their dad. Not really a precedent I want to set.

Sighing, I tilt my head back and gaze up at the ceiling. How am I going to navigate this whole thing with Garrett? I don't know if I can handle this for the next seven months.

A little bit of time passes with me sitting on the couch, my head spinning, before Garrett returns with a tray. He sets it next to me on the couch, and I peek at what he's made—a bowl of chicken noodle soup and a small plate of bread with jam.

"You had a can of soup in the pantry," he says. "I hope you don't mind that I dug around in there."

"I don't mind," I reply, picking up the bowl and sniffing it. When my stomach doesn't immediately pitch, I grab the spoon on the tray and slowly start eating. The soup is good. Soothing.

My stomach stays calm enough to finally put the food in it, and I realize just how hungry I've really been.

As I eat, Garrett moves around the living room and starts cleaning up. The place got a little cluttered when I wasn't feeling good, so there's dirty clothes lying on the floor, blankets in piles, empty or half-empty glasses of water, and unopened mail scattered around. He doesn't hesitate as he folds the blankets and gathers the clothes into a single pile. It's like he's done this a million times before, and it feels natural to have him here.

Too natural.

After several minutes, I can't stand the strained atmosphere between us anymore.

"What do you think of all this?"

He freezes in the middle of folding a large, patchwork quilt my mom made me when I was a kid. He appears thoughtful, as if choosing his words carefully.

"I'm stunned," he finally confesses. "I'm still processing everything and what this will mean for our lives. I know I'll love the baby, and a part of me is excited to be a dad. I also know I'll do everything I can to support you and the baby. You don't ever have to worry about that."

Again, he's saying all the right things. However, he doesn't say anything about what his feelings for me are, nor does he ask me what I feel for him... or about any of this, really.

"That's... good to know," I say. Garrett gives me a small half-smile before continuing to tidy up.

God, is this how it's going to be? Me tiptoeing around my real feelings while he caters to me, oblivious to the turmoil swirling within me, which only makes me feel shittier. He seems at ease and content with all this, but how long will that last? What if he comes to resent me for this? It's not like I got pregnant on purpose - I didn't magically make the condom break -

but that might not matter when he realizes just how much this will change his life.

A knock on my front door jerks me out of my racing thoughts. Who could that be? Frowning, I move to get off the couch, but Garrett quickly steps in front of me.

"I'll get it. Don't worry."

I don't have the energy to argue with him, so I sink back against the couch and let him go to the door.

"Oh, Garrett, what are you doing here?"

I recognize the voice instantly and tense. It's Meredith, and by the sound of the tiny footsteps rushing into the house, she's brought the littles with her. Damn it...I should've suspected she'd hunt me down when I ignored her calls.

Meredith, my youngest brother and sister, and Ally come walking into the living room.

"Hi, Marie!" My little sister, Avery, hurries to my side, jumping on the couch next to me.

"Hey, little lady," I reply, giving her a weak smile.

"Mommy said you were in the hospital," my brother, Henry, declares. "Were you sick?"

"I was, but I'm feeling much better now."

"I was so relieved to hear that you were able to come home," Meredith says. "The kids have been wanting to see you, so I thought I'd bring them by. I actually need you to watch them for a bit, so it's perfect. Ally tagged along to help you out."

I blink, stunned. Ally is standing next to her mom, her eyes downcast and her cheeks flushed, clearly embarrassed.

"Mom, I told you, I can watch the kids myself," Ally murmurs. "We don't need to bother Marie. She's still recovering..."

Meredith waves a hand dismissively and insists, "Oh, there's no need to worry. She's just pregnant, that's all. Of course,

Marie is happy to watch them. She's always happy to help out her family."

I'm absolutely speechless. Is she being serious? I just got out of the hospital, for fuck's sake. Does she seriously expect me to...

"I'm sorry, Meredith," Garrett says in a polite tone, stepping between me and my stepmother. "Marie won't be able to watch the kids today. She's too tired and still recovering. She needs to rest."

My heart flutters a little bit at his protectiveness, and I can't even make myself care that he's doing it out of obligation. Actually, maybe that's not true. He's stood up for me before against Meredith... I wasn't pregnant then.

He does care about me. Just not in the way I wish he would.

Unlike last time, Meredith doesn't seem at all charmed by him. Her brow furrows and her lips part.

"I beg your pardon?" she snaps. "Who do you think you are? This is a family matter. It has nothing to do with you."

"Actually, it does," Garrett insists in a firmer tone. "I don't mean to be rude, ma'am, but I'm going to have to set some ground rules regarding Marie. From now on, you will have to find a different babysitter. Marie won't be watching your children for you, unless you call well ahead to ask her and she agrees to because she wants to. All right?"

Holy shit. He's really laying down the law, and I... I don't hate it. Just like when he stood up for me in the library, I'm a bit overwhelmed by how good it feels to have someone actually on my side.

"You... you..." Meredith sputters, clearly struggling to come up with a response. It's not often she doesn't get her way. At length, she gets so frustrated that she literally stomps her foot and declares, "Fine! I'm not going to argue about this right now. I have more class than that. Come on, kids. Let's not disturb Marie any further."

"Get better soon, Marie," Avery says.

"Love you!" Henry chirps, making me feel a small tinge of guilt, but neither of them seem all that upset that I'm not going to watch them.

Meredith turns on her heel and storms out of the house in a huff, the kids and Ally following close behind her. I don't miss Ally's amused grin before she disappears from sight.

Garrett sees them out and when he comes back, he's shaking his head, his brow furrowed in annoyance.

"Geez, I don't know how you have the patience for that woman," he grumbles. "She gives me a headache." He stops when he's standing in front of me. "Are you okay?"

Nodding, I say, "I am. Thank you for standing up for me. I really appreciate it."

Honestly, it's a relief not to have to deal with Meredith right now with everything going on. I wouldn't have been able to stand up to her like that, so to have someone do it for me... to have Garrett looking out for my best interests... it's refreshing.

He gives me a soft smile. "I told you, I'm going to take care of you. All you need to worry about is getting well and taking care of yourself and the baby, okay?"

And there it is again... that mix of emotions I've been feeling since he walked into my hospital room a few days ago and after finding out I was pregnant.

I'm grateful for what he's doing for me. Taking care of me. Standing up for me. Making sure I'm focusing on my health and not putting too much stress on myself.

I'm also disappointed. I wish he was doing all this because he loved me. Because we're a couple and planning a future together. Anticipating raising this baby as a happy little family.

Instead, we're two people forced together by circumstances beyond our control. This isn't at all how I thought things would end up for me. That I'd end up with the man I love, but not because he loves me back, but because he's tethered to me for the rest of his life.

CHAPTER TWENTY-TWO
GARRETT

Over the next two weeks, I dedicate myself to caring for Marie, making sure she eats healthy meals that don't upset her stomach, gets a good amount of rest, and makes it to all her doctor appointments.

We fall into a routine. Every morning, I arrive at her house early to prepare breakfast because her morning sickness is particularly bad when she first wakes up. I'm there to make sure she's able to get out of bed and drinks plenty of water when she's done being sick. When she staggers out of the bathroom, pale and teary-eyed, my heart twists and I want to do whatever I can to make her feel better. Seeing her so miserable ruins me, and it kills me that I can't actually make her better.

My guilt eats me alive. I did this to her. She's going through this awful sickness and facing an uncertain future because I couldn't keep my desire for her under control. There's nothing I can do to make up for what that, so I'm doing everything in my power to make her comfortable. Whether it's running her errands or keeping her house tidy, I am her personal manservant.

It's really the least I can do for her. She's my responsibility now, as well as the baby. I'm not going to be the kind of guy who knocks up a woman and then abandons her because it's easier to walk away than stick around. Is this how I imagined starting a family? No. Do I feel ready to be a father? Not at all. But it's happening whether I'm ready or not, and I'm not going to leave Marie to deal with this alone.

One morning, I step inside the front door and can hear her in the bathroom upstairs. Rushing up the stairs, I find her kneeling on the floor, her head in the toilet.

"Marie? Are you okay?"

"Do I fucking look okay?" she growls without lifting her head. "Get out!"

"All right, all right," I say, backing out into the hall. "I'll be downstairs if you need me, okay?"

She doesn't answer, but blindly feels around until she grabs a towel lying on the floor and chucks it at me.

I dodge it and hurry to go back downstairs. As I make my way into the kitchen to start her breakfast, I can't help my small smile. Not because I find any pleasure in her misery, but because she's comfortable enough with me to tell me to shove it. It's weird, I'll admit, but since I've started taking care of her, I've grown more attuned to her moods and have a better understanding of how her mind works.

Marie doesn't let just anyone know what she's really feeling. She's so worried about being a burden to anyone else that she will put on a smile when she's in agony to keep the people around her comfortable. If she's vulnerable, she's an inconvenience... at least in her mind.

She'll be vulnerable with me. She'll be cranky, sad, and honest about how she feels and what she wants. Does that mean she snaps at me when she's upset? Yes, but I'm okay with it.

It means she trusts me to actually care for her.

I pull a carton of eggs out of the fridge and a skillet out of a cupboard. As I scramble the eggs, my mind wanders about what will happen once the baby comes.

It still hasn't fully set in that I'm going to be a father, but I'm excited. Every day my excitement grows. I like the idea of being a father—playing with my kid, teaching them how to ride a bike, watching them grow into an actual person—I can't wait for it all. There's always been a part of me that's wanted to have kids, admittedly, not in such a complicated way.

My phone buzzes in my back pocket, pulling me from my musings. With one hand, I stir the eggs while grabbing my phone out with the other. It's an email from my school. My heart starts hammering as I open it and scan through the message.

> **Dear Mr. Young,**
> **Congratulations!**
> **We are pleased to inform you that you have successfully met all the academic and institutional requirements to graduate with your Bachelor of Science in Finance. This is a significant milestone, and we commend your dedication and hard work throughout your academic journey...**

I stare at the email for several seconds, letting the words fully sink in.

Holy shit... I did it. I did it!

After all these years, I've finally earned my degree. A sense of pride and accomplishment washes through me. I haven't really felt this way in a long time. When was the last time I truly accomplished something for myself? Something that I wanted and wasn't pursuing out of some sense of obligation or responsibility?

The skillet hisses, making me jump. I've stopped stirring Marie's eggs in my excitement. I quickly put my phone down and try to salvage the food. When they're finished, I grab a plate and as I'm scooping the eggs onto it, Marie walks into the kitchen.

"Hey," she says with a yawn, rubbing her eyes. "Sorry I was a bitch earlier."

"Don't worry," I reply, shooting her a grin. "I doubt I'd be all that chipper if I was puking my guts up first thing in the morning."

She gives me a weak smile and moves to sit at the kitchen table. I put the eggs in front of her, along with a glass of orange juice and a cup of herbal tea. Marie gazes down at the plate before letting out a groan.

"I don't know if I can eat anything today," she says, pushing the plate away from her.

"That's all right," I assure her. "At least drink the juice and tea. You can't let yourself get dehydrated again."

She grabs the juice, taking a sip. Taking the seat next to her, I pull the plate of eggs toward me. I figured out pretty quickly not to make too much food for her. If she doesn't eat it, I do. It's just one more routine that we've fallen into together.

"I got some good news," I say before scooping up some eggs into my mouth.

She arches a brow. "Oh? What's that?"

Pulling out my phone, I bring up the email from my school and hand her the device. She reads the message, her eyes going wide with excitement.

She looks back up at me and exclaims, "Oh my God! This is incredible, Garrett. Congratulations! We have to celebrate." She pauses and appears thoughtful before continuing, "I'm going to throw you a graduation party."

"You don't have to…"

"Don't even try to convince me not to," she states, handing my phone back to me. "I'm sick. You're supposed to let me do what I want."

Sighing, I shake my head. "I don't think that's how this works exactly, but… all right. If you really want to throw me a party, I won't stop you."

She claps her hands in delight, looking more energized than I've seen her in days. Her cheeks flood with color and her eyes sparkle, and as I gaze at her, desire stirs deep in my belly and my cock twitches. Fuck, I need to keep it together. I've been doing my best to suppress my lust so I can focus on her health and well-being, but it's still there, sizzling and waiting to be blown into an inferno.

Being so close to her… caring for her… it's only made my feelings for her deepen, regardless of how determined I've been to try and put things back the way they were before. As she excitedly chatters away, talking about all the ideas she has for my party, I can only sit and watch her, knowing that I've been pushing myself to the edge of my control… and it's just a matter of time before the tether finally snaps.

***

A FEW DAYS LATER, I'm back at Marie's with groceries and more exciting news. After telling Christian that I'm officially graduating, he offered me a job at the new offices he's set up in Blue Ridge Falls in the finance department. Obviously, I accepted. The first person I wanted to tell was Marie… even more so than Haven. That realization left me a bit stunned.

Balancing the grocery bags in one arm, I open the front door of her house and walk inside.

"Marie!" I call out, kicking the door shut behind me. "I went to the store and picked up a few things to make you dinner. I've got some exciting news…"

I freeze when Marie walks down the stairs… wearing nothing but a towel. Her hair is wet and I can smell the scented lotion she always puts on after a shower. She stops and looks at me, her eyes going wide.

"Garrett! I didn't know when you were stopping by. I'm sorry, I was just going into the kitchen to look for my phone…"

She's startled and babbling, but I'm hardly listening. I can't tear my eyes from her. Her towel leaves little to the imagination. She's not showing yet, but my gaze drops to her belly and the thought of her pregnant with my child and standing nearly naked in front of me causes something in me to snap. Dropping the grocery bags on the floor, I stride toward her. She stares at me in shock but doesn't try to resist when I wrap my arms around her waist and pull her tight against me.

Her lips part on a gasp, and I catch them in a hard and hungry kiss. She wraps her arms around my neck and I pick her up, cupping her ass in both hands. We don't break our kiss as I carry her up the stairs and down the hall to her bedroom.

"Garrett," she murmurs when I set her down on the bed. "Are you sure…?"

One of my hands cups her face while the other yanks the towel off her.

"I'm really fucking sure," I growl.

"Good," she says, her voice breathless. Sliding her fingers into my hair, she yanks me back down to her lips. We fall back on the bed as we kiss, and I run my hands along her body. She's so soft. So curvy. Her breasts are fuller, her hips more luscious.

I trace my fingers over her still-flat belly, feeling a strange, primal desire rush through me.

To my surprise, she bats my hand away and breaks the kiss, turning her head as her cheeks turn dark pink.

Confused, I sit back on my knees above her. "What's wrong?"

She won't look at me as she nibbles on her bottom lip.

At length, she answers, "I'm... I'm afraid of getting too big."

I blink, stunned. "Too big? What are you talking about?"

Groaning, she finally meets my gaze. "My stomach is... ugh, God. What if you don't think I'm attractive when my stomach is huge?"

She waves her hands up and down over her body. I grab her wrists to stop her and gently pin her arms to the bed on either side of her head.

"You don't think you'll still be sexy when you're showing?"

"Please," she grumbles. "You don't have to pretend to make me feel better."

"Marie," I let go of her hands and drag my fingers down her torso to her stomach, "I'm so fucking turned on by your body, I could come in my pants, and I can guarantee you that's not going to change when your stomach grows."

Her jaw drops, and she gazes up at me, clearly shocked.

"Really?" she gasps.

I grab one of her hands and press it to the front of my pants. Her fingers curl around my already hardened cock and I let out a hiss of breath.

"Yeah, really."

She swallows and bites her bottom lip as she strokes me through my pants.

"You think I'm sexy," she whispers, more to herself really than to me.

I bend to press my lips to hers. "You're the sexiest woman I've ever met."

We're kissing again and the tension melts from her body. I tear my shirt off and throw it to the floor. Before I can undo my pants, Marie presses her hand to my chest and pushes me over and onto my back. She moves to sit on her knees between my legs and quickly works my pants open.

"Marie, you..."

"Shhh," she murmurs, pulling my hardening cock out. "Let me make you feel good."

Before I can say another word, she takes my shaft into her mouth and sucks me deep. I groan, clutching at the bedsheets as she bobs her head up and down.

"Holy shit..."

This feels incredible. The pleasure is overwhelming and I'm in danger of hitting my peak way too fast. I want to be inside her first.

"Marie," I groan. "Get on top. Ride me."

She lifts her head and gazes at me with shiny, hungry eyes. Nodding, she moves up my body and straddles my hips. Pressing her hands against my chest, she slowly lowers herself onto my cock. We both moan in pleasure.

"Oh, God," she whimpers.

I look up at her, my blood hot and my stomach tightening. She's so beautiful sitting on me with her belly and breasts on full display. I'm going to lose my goddamn mind.

Holding onto her thighs, I flex my hips, driving myself deeper into her. Marie cries out and then begins to ride me, undulating her hips back and forth. She sets the pace and moves faster and faster, growing as desperate for release as I am.

"Marie, I'm almost there," I growl.

"Me too," she gasps.

I press my thumb to her clit and rub, wanting her to hit her peak first. She lets out a cry, throwing her head back as her body seizes. She clenches around my cock as she comes and I can't hold back anymore. My orgasm explodes through me. Arching my back, I hold on tight to her hips as I pump into her over and over again. Stars explode in my vision, and I swear to God, I leave my body entirely.

When I come back, Marie is slumped against my chest, breathing heavily. I wrap my arms around her and hold her tight, not wanting to let her go yet. I'm afraid that once I do, I might regret this, and I don't want to. I want to cling to her for as long as I can before the guilt returns and pushes everything else away.

CHAPTER TWENTY-THREE
MARIE

I'm cozy and warm, and there's something strong and solid wrapped around me.

Slowly, my eyes open and I'm lying in Garrett's arms. The morning sun peaks through the curtains. Garrett is still asleep, and I gaze at his peaceful face as the events of the night play through my mind. He made me feel so incredible... sexy and desired, and the pleasure was mind blowing.

How could he ever doubt the chemistry between us? How good we are together?

Raising my hand, I lightly brush my fingers down his cheek. He stirs and opens his eyes. I'm not sure he knows where he is. I watch as realization comes over him, and with it, a flash of guilt.

Oh, no... please, no.

"Good morning," I say, my stomach twisting with anxiety.

Garrett disentangles himself from me and sits up. He won't look me in the eyes, and drops his head into his hands. I move to sit up next to him, clutching the blankets to my chest. I need something to act as a shield.

His shoulders tense and when I reach out to lay a hand on

his back, he flinches away from me. I blink, jerking my hand back, hurt by his rejection to my touch.

"I'm sorry," he says, shaking his head. "Fuck, Marie, I'm so sorry. We can't keep doing this…"

"Why?" Annoyance and frustration bubbles up and overflows into my voice. "Why do you keep pulling away like this when you know we're so good together?"

He doesn't answer. Instead, he pushes the blankets aside and moves to get out of the bed, grabbing his pants and yanking them on.

Oh, no. He's not getting out of this conversation that easily. I'm sick of him doing this to me, and I'm not going to let him go without giving me a damn explanation for once.

Grabbing his arm, I stop him and tug on him until he turns back around to me.

"Garrett, I am pregnant with your child! You made me promise that I woundn't keep any more secrets from you, and you need to do the same. You need to start being honest with me right the hell now."

He gazes at me, appearing surprised. I maintain eye contact, not willing to give him an inch of leeway.

At length, he releases a long sigh and hesitantly says, "All right… I… I made a promise to my mom."

I furrow my brow. "A promise? What kind of promise?"

"That I'd look after you just like I would Haven. Like you're my sister. To protect you and keep you safe. Every time I touch you, I'm breaking that promise."

I stare at him, stunned. That's why he won't be with me? After all this time, he's denying us because he is stuck with some weird notion that he's supposed to treat me like a sister?

"Are you kidding me?"

"I'm serious," he says. "I don't want to do anything to hurt you…"

"That's what you're doing now!" I insist, throwing the blankets aside and getting out of bed. I hurry to grab my robe off the back of the door and throw it on. "Do you really think your mother would want you to deny your own happiness? Would she be pleased to know that holding on to this promise is only causing me agony?"

He goes still and stares at me, looking absolutely dumbfounded.

"I... I never considered that possibility before," he murmurs.

Of course he hadn't. He's so focused on doing what he thinks is best, he is completely oblivious to what is actually happening around him.

My emotions are so overwhelming that I can hardly look at him anymore.

"I need you to leave."

"What?"

"I need space right now," I say, crossing my arms over my chest. "I have to think about everything... alone. Please, leave."

He hesitates and looks as though he wants to say something. A part of me hopes he'll ask to stay and tell me how much he wants me, but he doesn't.

Releasing a long sigh, he finishes getting dressed and leaves without a word.

LATER THAT DAY, I drive to Haven's house, my heart aching and confusion making my head foggy. After Garrett left, I texted Haven asking if we could meet, knowing she's not working Saturdays. I need to talk to someone; my best friend. She might be able to help me sort through whatever it is that Garrett is going through. Why he would think his promise to their mom meant that he couldn't be with me?

When I pull up to the house, Haven is already standing on the porch, waiting for me with a concerned frown. I park and get out of the car, rushing up the steps to her. She opens her arms and I throw myself into her embrace, careful not to disturb her belly too much.

"Hey," she says, pulling back and cupping my face in both her hands. "What's going on? Your text worried me."

"Can we go inside and talk? Christian's not here, is he?"

She shakes her head. "No, no, it's just us. He had to go into the office, which I'm not exactly complaining about - he's gotten used to me being pregnant enough that he doesn't feel the need to constantly be around me. Oliver is taking a nap so we can talk in private. Come on in."

Taking my hand, she turns and pulls me into the house. We make our way into the living and settle on the couch together.

Squeezing my hands, Haven says, "Okay, tell me... what's going on?"

I don't really know where to start, so I just take a deep breath and confess, "Garrett and I slept together last night."

Haven's eyes go wide. "You did? Is that... is that a good thing?"

"It's a complicated thing." I shake my head. "He told me why he's so insistent that we can't be together, though."

"Oh! What did he say?"

I hesitate, choosing my words carefully.

"He said he made a promise to your mom... to care for me like he would you. Like a sister. He thinks if he's with me... if he touches me, he's breaking that promise."

Haven arches her brows, looking stunned. Then she groans and shakes her head in obvious annoyance.

"First of all... that's disturbing for him to even say that. Because he clearly got you pregnant, so to still see you like a sister. My brother clearly has fucking issues. That I'm going to have to work with him on. Second off, he's a complete idiot sometimes," she grumbles, running a hand over her belly. "He takes things so literally."

"You don't think that's what your mom really meant?"

Haven rolls her eyes. "No, I don't think that. Of course, Mom wouldn't want the two of you to go through this turmoil. What she cared about most was that we were all happy and together. I have absolutely no doubt that if she knew you and Garrett had feelings for each other, she would want you to pursue them."

I don't know what to say. It's a relief to hear her agree with me, but that doesn't mean Garrett's mind will change. He's so determined to keep his promise as he understands it, that he's denying both of us what we really want... and I'm pregnant! I would think that would qualify as a good reason to put aside his hesitations and be with me.

And yet, he clings onto that promise. Too afraid to let his mother down than acknowledge my feelings, and his.

Shit... I'm never going to convince him that it's okay for us to be together?

As if she can read my mind, Haven grabs my hand again and squeezes it.

"Hey, don't worry," she says firmly. "We'll figure this out. I'll talk to Garrett myself. Convince him that he's misunderstood what Mom meant. You two are meant to be together, Marie. I know it."

If only I had her confidence, but it's getting harder and harder to convince myself that's true. There's no one in the world I want more than Garrett, but it's not just the two of us anymore. I have to think of the baby and what will be best for him or her in the long term. How healthy would it be for my child to watch their parents dance around our issues like this? What will I tell them when they inevitably ask why I'm not with their father? Am I supposed to say that daddy doesn't want to be with mommy because of a promise he made to their grandma before she died? That their father thinks loving me is wrong?

It's a gut wrenching thought, and I can't put either the baby or myself through that.

"I appreciate the offer to talk to Garrett," I tell Haven with a resigned sigh. "But I don't think it'll do any good."

"You can't give up," she insists. "Just leave it to me. Trust me, okay?"

I give her a small, sad smile. "I trust you more than anyone, Haven. I know you'll try your hardest, but I'm not sure I can afford to hold onto hope for much longer."

Haven gives me a sympathetic look before pulling me into another hug. I sink into her embrace, grateful for her care and concern. I know, no matter what happens between me and Garrett, that I'll always have her. She'll always be my family.

I don't realize I'm crying until we pull apart and Haven gets a good look at my face.

She gasps. "Oh, honey! Don't cry."

"I'm okay," I softly sob.

"Ugh, if I weren't a big as a fucking whale, I'd hunt Garrett down and kick his ass myself," Haven huffs. Then, in a softer tone, "No matter what happens, you're not going to be alone, okay?"

"I know. Thank you, Haven. I don't know what I'd do without you."

She cups my face and wipes away my tears with her thumb. "Don't worry. You're never going to have to find out."

Despite everything, that does bring me a bit of comfort. Even if Garrett can never see what's standing right in front of him, Haven will always see me.

I just wish he could do the same.

CHAPTER TWENTY-FOUR
GARRETT

My new office still has the faint smell of fresh paint, and everything in it is shiny and new; the dark wooden desk, the desktop computer with its two monitors, and the empty bookshelves that I've been slowly filling up with books and binders filled with company invoices and financial excel sheets from past years.

Christian really hooked me up, making sure I have every supply and software I'll need for my new job. Honestly, a part of me thinks he's more excited for this than I am, and I'm thrilled. This is exactly the sort of career I'd always imagined for myself—a corner office, my own assistant at her desk outside my door, and no fear of accident or injury while on the job. It's only been a few days since I've started, so I'm still getting settled in and used to everything, but I'm feeling good about this new start.

Unfortunately, that's about the only thing I feel good about right now. It's been nearly a week since I was with Marie, and we haven't spoken since. I've sent her a few texts, just to try and check in, but the only response she ever sent was her repeating that she needs time and space. I'm trying to give that to her, but it's difficult. I'm torn between my lingering guilt about my promise to Mom and my feelings for Marie. I want to fix things between us, but I have no idea how to do that. Still, knowing she's upset with me, and knowing I deserve it is something I hate more than anything. I've done nothing but screw up her life and break her heart.

Sighing, I sit back in my chair and scrub a hand over my mouth. This isn't going to work. I can't focus on my job because of my anxiety about Marie, and I don't want Christian to kick my ass out of here and back to the oil fields.

As my mind is spinning with everything going on with Marie, my cellphone buzzes on my desk. It's Haven. With a frown, I answer it.

"Hey," I say. "What's up?"

"Garrett, you and I need to have a conversation," she answers. "Are you free after work today?"

"Uh, yeah. Is everything okay?"

"I'm fine," she assures me. "But we have some things we need to discuss, and they're important. Meet me at the coffee shop when you get off."

It doesn't escape me that she's not making a request. "All right, I'll be there."

"See you later."

She hangs up without a goodbye, leaving me caught off guard and confused from her curt tone. Crap, she didn't sound exactly happy. What could she want to talk about?

I can't help but feel like my ass is about to be chewed, and I'm afraid to find out why.

AFTER WORK, I head straight to the coffee shop. Haven is already here, sitting at a table in the far corner. I make my way over to her and she looks up, her brow furrowed. She looks irritated as I sit down across from her.

"Hey," I cautiously say. "What's going on?"

She narrows her eyes and snaps, "Do you really think you're keeping your promise to Mom by breaking Marie's heart over and over?"

"What? Marie told you…"

"Whatever you think, you're not," she continues, cutting me off. "This isn't what Mom would've wanted at all."

I bristle at her words, but ready to defend myself. "I know that you think I'm being ridiculous, but I'm just trying to do the right thing and honor Mom's memory by keeping my distance from Marie. Mom thought of her as a second daughter… she would've been disappointed to know that I don't think of Marie as a sister."

Haven rolls her eyes and lets out a huff of breath. "Do you hear yourself? Yes, Mom treated Marie like she was part of the family, but that doesn't make her your sister in any sort of capacity. Mom wouldn't have wanted you to sacrifice your own happiness or cause Marie so much pain."

Her words hit me hard. Marie said something similar the other morning and they shocked me then as well. Guilt and confusion roll through me, mixing together into a toxic sludge in my stomach. Slowly, I shake my head.

"A-a relationship with Marie would be a mistake. I'm supposed to protect her and look out for her. Not take advantage…"

"Being in a relationship with her wouldn't mean you're taking advantage of her," Haven says, her tone gentler but still firm. "Garrett, just think about this for a minute, okay? Are you really taking care of Marie this way? Protecting her? Or are you causing more harm than good? Would Mom actually be happy with this situation?"

A part of me wants to latch onto what she's saying and give into all the desire and want that has been building inside of me for Marie, but another part of me insists that I can't. Crossing the line with Marie would be a betrayal of Mom, and I can't just let that belief go so easily. It's been such a defining aspect of my life since Mom passed. So many of my decisions have been made with that promise in mind.

The idea that I've misinterpreted what Mom wanted all this time is gut-wrenching.

Meeting Haven's gaze, I say, "How do you know that's not what Mom wanted?"

She frowns and shakes her head. "Mom only ever wanted us to be happy, Garrett. Come on, do you really think she'd be upset if you were with Marie? Hell, if you two got married, Marie would have been her daughter for real. I don't think much of anything would have pleased her more."

I can't deny that Haven has a point there, and I hadn't thought about that before. Have I really been so wrong all this time? Did I take Mom's words too literally?

"Garrett, what do you want? Don't think about your promise to Mom. Just tell me what it is you really want."

The answer comes easily, it's not something I even have to think about.

"I want Marie," I confess softly.

Haven gives me a small, encouraging smile. "Does Marie make you happy?"

When I spend time with her, it's the highlight of my whole day. Her smile is infectious, and the sound of her laugh is enchanting. Of course she makes me happy. Even though I've been riddled with guilt, the moments wrapped in her arms, her body pressed to mine, have been some of the most satisfying of my life.

"Yes," I murmur. "She makes me happy."

"Okay then, last question. If Mom were alive, would she be happy if you and Marie were together?"

I freeze as the question swirls in my brain. Fuck, it's so obvious, isn't it?

"She'd be thrilled."

Haven's right... Mom wouldn't be upset at all if Marie and I were together. I can almost see her, happy tears in her eyes as she hugs us and tells us how much she loves the both of us.

My breath leaves me in a rush. Relief rushes through me, but apprehension as well. I've messed things up so badly... what if Marie has already given up on me?

"You need to talk to Marie," Haven says, reaching across the table and taking my hand. "You need to tell her how you really feel."

Looking at our entwined hands makes me realize how dumb I've been. Haven has always been there for me, and not coming to her sooner was stupid. Yet, I can't help the doubt that plagues me. "What if she doesn't believe me? She'll think I'm just trying to stay close to her because of the baby if I show up and completely change my tune about the two of us."

"Then you need to prove to her that you care about her as a person and not just because she's having your baby," Haven states matter-of-factly.

"How?"

She shrugs. "That's something you have to figure out for yourself. What's something that you could do that would leave no doubt in her mind that you have genuine feelings for her?"

"I-I'm not sure."

She sighs and pushes to her feet, struggling a bit as she finds her balance with her belly.

"Give it some thought." She moves around the table and places a kiss on the top of my head. "Whatever you figure out, make sure it actually means something to her, okay? It has to have an impact."

She puts a hand on my shoulder and squeezes before walking away and out of the shop.

I watch her through the front window and suddenly, Christian appears, popping out from around the shop's corner. Haven is obviously surprised, jumps, smacks him on the shoulder, and scolds him, though I can't tell what she's saying. However, the next moment, she grabs the front of his shirt and pulls him down into a kiss before smacking him again. He grins sheepishly, and the two start heading down the sidewalk together and out of sight.

Shaking my head, I chuckle and settle back in my chair. Alone with my thoughts, I still have no idea what kind of gesture would be grand enough to prove my feelings to Marie, but I'm determined to figure it out.

I DON'T STAY MUCH LONGER at the coffee shop. As I drive home, the passing scenery barely registers. My mind is elsewhere, turning over every idea, every possible way to show Marie that I care. She deserves more than an apology. She deserves proof that I'm all in.

As I pass through downtown, a familiar building catches my eye. The bookstore. Marie's bookstore.

That's it!

I nearly miss my turn as the idea takes shape. If reopening her mom's shop is Marie's dream, then what better way to show her how much she means to me than by helping her make it happen?

By the time I pull into my driveway, my heart is pounding

with a mix of nerves and excitement. I sit in the truck, staring at the house but not really seeing it.

Can I actually do this? It's not like I have experience with bookstores or renovations, but I know people who do. Mason, with his contractor business and experience, could be perfect to help me with this plan.

I pull out my phone and scroll to his number. The line rings twice before his familiar, laid-back voice answers.

"Garrett? What's up, man?"

"Mason, I need your help," I say, skipping the small talk.

There's a pause on the other end. "Okay... what kind of help are we talking about?"

"Marie's mom's old boutique," I say, the words tumbling out in a rush. "I want to renovate it. Fix it up. She's been wanting to do it for years, but has never had the time or the money."

"Wait, are you serious?" Mason sounds more intrigued than skeptical, which is a good sign.

"Dead serious. I don't know the first thing about restoring a shop, but I know you do. I'll pay you for your time, whatever it takes."

"We'll figure all that out, don't you worry," Mason says, chuckling. "I'll give you the friends and family discount or something. But you've got to tell me—why the sudden interest in this place?"

"Because I care about her. And I need to prove it to her in a way that matters."

There's a beat of silence, and then Mason finally opens his mouth. "All right. I'm in. When do we start?"

A wave of relief washes over me. "Tomorrow, if you're free. I'll meet you at the shop, and we can take a look at what needs to be done."

"Sounds good. I'll bring my tools and coffee. We're going to need it."

I hang up, feeling a flicker of hope for the first time in days. It's not much yet, just the spark of an idea, but it's something.

As I head inside, I can't stop thinking about how Marie's face might light up when she sees the shop restored. If I can pull this off, maybe it'll be enough to show her how much she means to me—and that I'm finally ready to let go of the past for a chance at a future with her.

CHAPTER TWENTY-FIVE
MARIE

The clouds hang low and heavy in the sky as I steer my car toward Haven's house. The grayness outside feels like a reflection of the fog that's settled in my mind these last few days. Garrett hasn't called and hasn't texted, and to be fair, I haven't reached out to him either. Still, after Haven promised to talk to him, I was half-expecting that he'd reach out and apologize or something.

Instead, the silence between us stretches longer with every passing hour, and with it, my hope dwindles. I haven't even had the heart to throw him the graduation party I promised - it just feels weird to do so when things between us are so strained.

I shouldn't have expected more from him. He's so wrapped up in that damn promise... I don't stand a chance against his determination to keep it. As he understands it, at least. The thought makes my heart twist. I push it away, focusing instead on the winding road ahead. I need to talk to Haven again and find out how her conversation with Garrett went. If she thinks there's still hope, maybe I won't give up... but if she doesn't...

When I pull into the driveway, I try to shake off the weight of the anxiety pressing down on me. Haven's car is in the driveway, but something doesn't feel right... the house looks still—too still. The curtains are drawn, no lights shine through the windows, and I can't hear any music or voices from inside. Something is definitely off.

I step out of the car, my footsteps crunching on the gravel as I approach the front door.

When I knock, no one answers. A sense of unease settles over me.

Trying the doorknob, I find it unlocked.

Opening the door, I call out, "Haven? It's me, Marie."

Silence.

My unease deepens. The house feels unnaturally quiet. My sneakers squeak against the hardwood floor as I make my way into the living room. No sign of her there.

What's going on? I'm seized by a sense of foreboding.

"Haven, where are you?" My voice wavers as I walk toward the stairs. A faint groan reaches my ears, stopping me dead in my tracks. I freeze, straining to hear over the pounding of my heart.

Another sound—this time clearer—comes from upstairs. A second groan. It sounds painful.

Panicked, I bolt up the steps two at a time, my breath catching in my throat. "Haven!"

The groans grow louder as I approach the bedroom. Pushing the door open, Haven sits on the edge of the bed, her face pale and shiny with sweat. One hand clutches her abdomen, and the other grips the edge of the mattress. Her breathing is labored, and her eyes, wide with fear, meet mine. Relief washes over her face, but it's fleeting, quickly replaced by a grimace of pain.

"Marie," she whispers, her voice strained. "Oh, thank God!"

I rush to her side, dropping my bag to the floor. "Haven! What's happening? Where's Christian?"

She groans and rolls her eyes. "Oh, he had a work emergency in Houston. He wasn't going to go, but I convinced him that he should and I'd be okay, so of course this happens..."

My gaze falls to her belly. "Are you—"

She cuts me off with a gasp. "I think... I think it's time."

My stomach flips. "Oh my God. Okay. Okay, um..." I look around the room, my thoughts racing. I have to keep my cool. No matter what, anxiety and fear can't overwhelm me because that's not going to help Haven. Still, I wasn't expecting this. The baby isn't due for a few more weeks...

"You're early," I blurt out.

"I know!" she snaps, her voice laced with panic and pain. "Tell the baby that!"

"Right. Sorry." I take a deep breath, trying to focus. "We need to get you to the hospital. Can you walk?"

Haven shakes her head, biting her lip as another contraction takes hold. She leans forward, her whole body trembling as she lets out a strangled cry. Fuck, fuck, fuck! She's in so much pain!

I grab her hand, squeezing it tightly. "I'm here, okay? We're going to get through this."

The words tumble out because I have no idea what else to say. How are we going to get through this? Doesn't matter, I'm going to do everything to help her right now.

She nods weakly, tears glistening in her eyes.

"Where's Oliver?" I ask.

"With my step-dad," she groans. "Christian called him when he finally decided to leave town...asked him to watch him so I could rest. We need to let Peter know what's going on."

"We will, we will," I assure her, scanning the room. "Do you have a hospital bag packed?"

"Closet," she manages through gritted teeth.

I dart across the room, yanking open the closet door. A small duffel bag sits on the floor, ready and waiting. I grab it and sling it over my shoulder.

Returning to the bed, I take hold of her and help her to her feet.

"Here we go. One foot in front of the other, yeah? I'm going to get you down to my car."

Haven clutches my arm as we make our way out of the bedroom and reach the top of the stairs. Her breathing is shallow and uneven, and her grip tightens as another contraction ripples through her body. Her nails dig into my skin and bite back the sting and panic rising in my throat. Focus. Just focus. Get her out of the house and into the car and go from there. Stay focused.

"Christian," Haven gasps between breaths. "You...you have to call Christian...."

My heart skips a beat, but I force a reassuring smile. "It's okay. We'll get you to the hospital, and I'll work on trying to contact him. Right now, you are priority one."

She leans against me for support. "I can't believe this is happening now."

"Me neither," I admit, trying to inject a touch of humor into my voice. "But hey, this baby's got its own timeline. Let's just roll with it, okay?"

Haven manages a faint smile, but her eyes are clouded with fear. I don't blame her. Inside, I'm a mess of nerves. The baby is early. What does that mean? Is something wrong? Maybe it's because I'm pregnant now too, but this situation is freaking me out more than it should. It's unlocking fears within me that I'm not sure how to deal with. So much can go wrong in a pregnancy.

What if something goes wrong with mine?

"Let's take it slow," I say, guiding her down the stairs as I push my spinning thoughts aside. With one arm wrapped securely around her waist, she grips the railing with her free hand, and step by step, we make our way down. My breath catches each time she pauses, bracing herself against another contraction. The tension in her body is palpable, and I feel it echoing in my own muscles.

"Almost there," I murmur, more to myself than to her.

By the time we reach the bottom, we're both trembling. Haven sinks onto the steps, as if she can't hold herself up anymore, and I kneel in front of her, brushing a stray strand of hair from her damp forehead.

"You're doing amazing," I say, even though she probably doesn't feel like it. "Just hang in there a little longer. We're almost on our way."

She nods, tears glistening in her eyes.

I give her a few seconds to catch her breath, but we can't linger here for too long.

"Ready?" I ask, my voice steady even though my heart is racing.

"As I'll ever be," she whispers.

Supporting her with both arms, I help her back to her feet. Together, we shuffle toward the door. The walk from the front door to my car feels like a marathon, but we keep pace as we shuffle along.

I unlock the car and open the passenger door, easing Haven into the seat. She winces as another contraction grips her, and I hold her hand until it passes.

"You're doing great," I tell her. "Just hang on a little while longer."

She gives me a faint smile. "Okay... I'll try. Thank you, Marie. I don't know what I'd have done if you hadn't shown up.."

"Don't thank me yet," I reply with a wry smile. "Let's get you to the hospital first."

I close her door gently and hurry around to the driver's side. Sliding into the seat, I start the car and glance over at her. She's taking deep breaths and seems to be putting all her focus into sucking air in and pushing air out.

"Ready to meet your baby?" I ask.

She nods, her expression a mixture of fear and determination.

With a deep breath, I pull out of the driveway. The car hums beneath us as we speed toward the hospital, my grip on the wheel tight enough to turn my knuckles white. Haven's shallow breathing fills the car, punctuated by sharper intakes of air every time another contraction hits.

"It's going to be okay," I say, half for her and half for myself.

"I... I need Christian."

"Don't worry, I'll make sure he knows." Grabbing my phone, I use voice commands to call Christian. It rings several times before going to his voicemail. Damn it! Come on, man. "Christian? This is Marie. Haven is in labor, and I'm taking her to the hospital. She needs you to head home, now!"

I hang up and try again, and again, no answer. Where is he that he's not seeing all these calls coming into his phone?

I glance over at Haven between calls, her face pale and drawn, her fingers gripping the seatbelt across her chest. I hit redial once more.

"Come on, Christian. Pick up."

For the fifth time, his voicemail clicks on. My frustration bubbles over, but I tamp it down. No time for that now. I wait for the beep and leave another message, keeping my voice calm but firm.

"Christian, it's Marie again. Come on, man. Haven needs you. Call me as soon as you get this!"

I hang up and Haven gasps, "Try his assistant, Laura." She rattles off a number, and I connect the call.

Please answer.

On the second ring, she picks up, her tone brisk but professional. "This is Laura."

"Laura, it's Marie, a friend of Haven's. I'm trying to reach Christian, but he's not answering. Haven's in labor, and we're heading to the hospital now. Can you get a hold of him?"

There's a brief pause, and then she says, "Oh my—okay, I'll track him down right away. Do you know which hospital?"

"Blue Ridge Falls Medical. Please, Laura, it's urgent."

"I'll take care of it. Thank you for letting me know," she replies before the call ends.

"We're almost there, Haven," I say, glancing at her. She's biting her lip, her eyes squeezed shut against the pain, my heart pounding as the hospital's lights come into view.

I pull up to the emergency room entrance and throw the car into park. Jumping out, I rush to Haven's side and help her out.

We make our way inside, and a nurse at the front desk looks up.

"She's in labor!"

Within moments, a team of nurses arrives with a wheelchair. They take Haven from my arms, moving quickly but gently. I follow closely, clutching the hospital bag, my adrenaline spiking.

Haven's gaze locks onto mine as they wheel her toward the maternity ward.

"Marie," she whispers, her voice shaky. Scared. "I can't do this alone."

My heart hurts and I force a reassuring smile as I hurry to keep up with her.

"I'm right here. "I'm not going anywhere."

The nurses guide us into a delivery room. Haven clutches the side rails of the bed as another contraction hits, her face contorting with pain.

"You're doing great," I say, brushing her hair back from her damp forehead. "You're so strong, Haven. Just keep breathing."

Her grip on my hand tightens. I stay by her side, murmuring encouragement as the medical team moves around us, preparing for the baby's arrival.

Through it all, my phone stays silent. No call from Christian, no word from Laura. I fight the urge to check it every five seconds, keeping my focus on Haven. Right now, she's all that matters.

CHAPTER TWENTY-SIX
GARRETT

The air inside the old bookstore is heavy with dust and smells musty, but I can already see the potential. Mason stands next to me, tapping a pencil against a clipboard as we go over the list of repairs we've come up with.

"We'll need to start with the structural stuff," he says, pointing to a sagging beam near the back. "Can't do anything else until we make sure the place won't collapse."

"Agreed," I reply, running my hand over a patch of peeling wallpaper. "Once that's done, we'll need to replace the flooring, repaint, and update the lighting. Marie's got a good eye for design—she'll know how to make this place shine."

Mason smirks. "You're really pulling out all the stops for her, huh?"

"Yeah," I admit, feeling a little sheepish but also determined. "I need her to know how much she means to me."

Renovating her mom's old store is the biggest, most meaningful gesture I can do for her. Helping her to achieve her greatest dream is how she'll know my feelings are real.

That's the hope, at least.

We're in the middle of measuring the back wall when my

phone buzzes in my pocket. I glance at the screen and see that Christian is calling. Odd... he's supposed to be in Dallas. I helped him prepare for his meetings, putting together charts to show the company's financial situation for him to show the board. Crap, did I forget something?

"Hang on," I tell Mason, answering the call. "Christian, what's up? Everything go okay with the board?"

His voice is frantic, words coming in bursts through a poor connection. "Garrett—Haven—hospital—labor—"

The line crackles, and I press the phone tighter to my ear. Did he say Haven?

"Christian, slow down. What's going on?"

"Marie—there—labor—early—"

The static cuts off the rest, but I hear enough. My stomach drops, and panic surges through me, making it hard to think straight. Marie. Labor. Fuck, is the baby coming? That can't be right! It's too soon. It's way too soon!

"I'm on my way," I say, ending the call before he can reply.

"Mason," I say, turning to him, my voice tight with urgency. "There's an emergency. I have to go."

"Wait—what's going on?" he asks, looking bewildered.

"No time to explain." I'm already heading for the door, my mind racing.

I get in my truck and take off for the hospital. I can barely see the road through the blur of terrified thoughts clouding my mind. Marie. Labor. Too early. My grip on the wheel tightens as I weave through traffic, pushing the speed limit but not caring. My heart is pounding so hard it feels like it might burst from my chest.

When I screech into the hospital, I barely register where I park. I'm out of the truck in seconds, sprinting toward the entrance.

The receptionist looks up, startled, as I barrel through the doors.

"Marie Green," I pant. "Where is she?"

"Marie Green?" she repeats, her fingers hovering over her keyboard.

"Yes!" I'm nearly shouting, my voice rough with panic. "She's in labor—where is she?"

The woman frowns, slightly confused. "Sir, I don't have a Marie Green listed in active labor."

My pulse spikes again. "I was told she was here—there has to be some mistake!"

"Calm down," she says, a little firmer this time. "If she's here, she might be in the maternity ward. Take the elevator to the third floor and check the waiting area."

I don't even thank her. I'm off toward the elevators, jamming the button repeatedly until the doors slide open. Every second feels like an eternity.

When I finally reach the third floor, I burst out into the corridor, scanning every face, every corner. My pulse roars in my ears as I turn down a hallway—and then I see her.

Marie.

She's sitting in a chair by herself, her face calm, her hands resting on her lap. She looks up, startled, when I come skidding to a halt in front of her.

"Garrett?" she asks, blinking in surprise. "What are you doing here?"

I stare at her, my chest heaving. Relief floods through me so fast I'm dizzy. She's fine. She's okay.

"You're not—" I start, but my voice cracks. "You're not in labor?"

Her brow furrows, and then her eyes widen in realization. "Oh, no! Garrett, no. I'm not in labor." She stands up quickly, placing a hand on my arm. "It's Haven. She's the one in labor. I've been here with her."

I stagger back a step, running a hand over my face as embarrassment washes over me. "I thought—Christian called—and it was static—and I heard your name—and labor—and—"

Marie's expression softens, a flicker of concern in her eyes.

"You thought it was me," she finishes, her voice gentle.

I feel like a complete idiot, but also overwhelmingly relieved. "I was terrified. I thought something had happened to you. To the baby."

Her hand squeezes my arm, grounding me. "I'm okay. I promise."

We just stand and stare at each other. I'm overwhelmed with everything I feel for this woman. When I thought she and the baby were in trouble, it was like my whole world was falling apart. Imagining my life without her... it shook me to my core.

I can't be without her. Marie is everything to me.

Clearing my throat, I murmur, "Marie, I..."

The doors to the maternity ward suddenly burst open, interrupting me, and Christian rushes in, wild-eyed. His tie is askew, his hair sticking up, and his face is flushed with worry. The instant he spots Marie and me, his shoulders sag in visible relief.

"Did I miss it?" he asks, his voice tight with panic as he jogs toward us.

Marie offers him a reassuring smile. "No, you made it. Haven's still in labor."

"Thank God." He presses his hands to his knees, catching his breath. Then he straightens and looks at me, clapping a hand on my shoulder. "Garrett. Thanks for being here."

I feel a pang of guilt for my earlier panic and misunderstanding. "Of course. I wouldn't let her do this alone."

Christian gives me a small, grateful smile before turning to Marie. "How's she doing? Is she okay?"

"She's doing great. The nurses say everything's progressing normally. She's a little early, but they're not worried."

Christian exhales deeply, muttering, "Thank God," again under his breath. Then he glances at the door leading to the delivery rooms. "Can I see her?"

Marie points down the hallway. "She's down in room 304. You should be able to get in when you tell them you're the father."

"All right, I'll check back in with you guys later." Christian dashes off down the hall and Marie and I are alone again. I look back at her, but her brow is furrowed, and she's clearly distracted by everything else going on. I swallow back the words I was going to say to her and tell myself to wait. Now's not the time.

So we wait.

The minutes stretch into an hour, then two. I pace the small waiting room while Marie sits quietly nearby, her hands rubbing her belly absently as she stares down the hallway toward Haven's room.

Finally, a nurse appears, and I stop moving, my heart in my throat.

"Miss Green and Mr. Young?" she asks, looking between us.

I nod. "Yes, that's us. Any news?"

The nurse smiles. "Mrs. Tallow has given birth to a healthy baby girl, and would like you two to come back and meet her."

Warm floods me and I stare at her, stunned.

Marie stands and comes up to my side, taking my arm. "Let's go see your new niece."

I let her lead me down the hall behind the nurse and we get to Haven's room. When we get inside, the scene before us stops me in my tracks. Haven is sitting up in the hospital bed, her face flushed but glowing with happiness. Christian is beside her, cradling a tiny bundle in his arms. He looks up as we enter, his face alight with pride.

"She's perfect," he says, looking up at us, his voice thick with emotion.

He steps forward, carefully placing the baby in Haven's arms. Haven looks down at her daughter with an expression of pure love and wonder.

Marie approaches the bed, leaning down to kiss Haven's forehead.

"She's beautiful, Haven," she says softly, her voice trembling.

Haven's gaze shifts to me.

"Garrett," she says, her voice tired but warm. "Come meet your niece."

I step forward hesitantly, my throat tightening as I look at the tiny, perfect face peeking out from the blanket. She's so small, so fragile, and yet, she's the most amazing thing I've ever seen. I'm overwhelmed with love for this little girl, so much so that my thoughts shift right to Marie and our baby.

If I feel this way at my niece's birth, what will I feel when my child is born?

Haven smiles up at me.

"Her name is Leila," she says. "Leila Tallow."

I swallow hard as I reach out to gently brush a finger against Leila's tiny hand. Tears well up in my eyes and my heart twists in my chest as I think of Mom and how much she would love this. I hear Marie let out a small sob, but I can't look away from Leila. She curls her fingers around mine, and I'm officially a goner.

WHEN VISITING HOURS ARE OVER, Marie and I leave the hospital together. We both hate to leave Haven, Christian, and Leila, but we know they all need their rest. Peter brought Oliver over earlier to meet his new sister, but took him back home already to get him fed and ready for bed. The hospital parking lot is quiet as Marie and I walk to my car. The glow of the streetlights reflects off her face, making her look soft and contemplative... but she also looks exhausted.

"Why don't I give you a ride home?" I say. "We can get your car tomorrow when we come back to visit."

She appears hesitant, but then sighs and nods. "Okay, that actually sounds good."

I lead her to my truck, unlock the door and hold it open for her. Once she's settled, I slide into the driver's seat, glancing at her out of the corner of my eye. I try to steady the nervous energy bubbling up inside me. Tonight has been overwhelming, in more ways than one, but I'm not ready to let this night end—not until I tell her everything.

"There's something I want to show you before I take you home," I say.

She tilts her head, curiosity flickering in her eyes. "What is it?"

"You'll see," I reply, starting the truck and pulling out of the parking lot.

The drive to the bookstore doesn't take long, but the tension in the car feels thick enough to cut with a knife. When we arrive, I park out front and get out, walking around to open her door.

She steps out slowly, her gaze darting to the dimly lit building. "Garrett.... Why are we here?"

"Don't be mad, but I asked Ally for a favor," I tell her, pulling a key out of my pocket. "She got me this so I could see what exactly we'd be working with."

My hands are steady as I unlock the door, and I gesture for her to step inside. The faint smell of mustiness and dust greets us and our footsteps on the worn floor.

Marie looks around, her expression a mixture of confusion and nostalgia. "I don't understand..."

Taking a deep breath, I steady myself. This is it.

"I've been working on a plan," I begin, my voice low but steady as I turn to face her. "To fix this place up for you."

Her head snaps toward me, her eyes wide. "What?"

I step closer. "I know how much this place means to you. I know how much your mom means to you, and I know how much you've wanted to reopen this place as your own."

She covers her mouth with her hand, and I can see tears forming in her eyes.

"Why would you do this?" she whispers.

I take another step forward, reaching out to gently take her hands in mine. "Because I've been an idiot, Marie. For so long, I let fear hold me back. I made a promise to my mom, and I thought honoring it meant shutting out my own happiness and resisting what I feel for you, but I was wrong."

Her hands tremble in mine, but she doesn't pull away.

"I love you," I confess, my voice thick with emotion. "I've loved you for a long time, and the thought of losing you, of pushing you away because of my own stupidity—it's unbearable. My mom wouldn't have wanted this. She wouldn't have wanted me to push away someone who makes me feel alive, who understands me, and who challenges me, and she wouldn't have wanted me to hurt you. She loved you and just wanted you to be happy, and I've been getting in the way of that by denying my feelings."

Tears spill down Marie's cheeks. "Garrett..."

I squeeze her hands gently. "I don't want to hide how I feel anymore. I want to build a life with you—not because I feel obligated, but because I choose you. More than anything in the world, I want to be with you. I want us to be a family, Marie. Please tell me it's not too late. That my foolishness hasn't pushed you away for good."

She doesn't say anything for several moments as she gazes at me, and I don't know what's going through her head. I've disappointed her before, so if she struggles to believe me now, it's understandable. If she doesn't, I won't give up.

I'm all in with her.

Moments pass, feeling like hours, before she finally replies, her lips trembling. "I love you too, Garrett. I always have."

Her words cause a weight to lift off my chest, and I pull her into my arms, holding her tightly. My heart feels like it's going to burst, it's beating so hard.

When she looks up at me, her dark brown eyes shining with tears and love, I kiss her. With the kiss, I make a silent vow to spend the rest of my life making up for all the hurt I've caused her. I'll never let her doubt my love and dedication to her ever again.

This is right. This is exactly where I'm supposed to be... in her arms, wrapped up in her love and the warmth of her touch.

When we finally pull apart, her forehead rests against mine, and she whispers, "I can hardly believe this is real."

I smile, brushing a tear from her cheek. "This is just the beginning, Marie. I promise."

CHAPTER TWENTY-SEVEN
MARIE

"Are you sure you want to do this?" Garrett asks as we walk down the street toward the bookstore.

I glance up at him and nod, clenching my teeth in determination.

"Yeah, yeah, this is important," I assure him. "I have to do this."

He gives me a nod and reaches down to place his hand on the small of my back. His touch is warm and firm and helps me keep my courage up. The boutique comes into sight a moment later, and my dad is waiting for us outside the front door. As we approach, he gives me a small, irritated frown.

"What am I doing here, Marie?" he demands to know without bothering to say hello. I knew asking him to meet me here would aggravate him - he hasn't stepped foot in this place since Mom died, and actually tried to convince me to sell it when I turned eighteen.

"You and I need to talk, Dad," I say, coming to a stop in front of him.

"And we have to talk here?" he grumbles, glancing up at the store front.

"Yeah," I nod. "We do. Come on in."

Stepping past him, I pull the key from my pocket and unlock the door. I walk inside and turn to make sure Dad follows me. It's a relief when he does and Garrett steps in after him, shutting the door behind him. Stopping in the middle of the space, I face Dad fully. He's gazing around with a scowl.

"This place is a dump," he declares. "Why do we have to do this here?"

Taking a deep breath, I raise my chin and say, "Because I'm going to reopen it as a bookstore. I've been wanting to for years and with Garrett's help, I'm finally going to do it."

Dad gives me a skeptical look before shooting a glare at Garrett.

"What? It's not enough you get my daughter pregnant, but you have to convince her to leave her stable job for this place?" Dad scoffs and shakes his head. "What a crock of shit."

I press my lips together as my anger rises up and burns through me.

"Dad, stop!" I snap. "Don't talk to Garrett like that. We're together, and he's the father of my baby. Show him some respect."

Dad rolls his eyes. "Marie, I don't have time for this. Tell me what I'm doing here or I'm leaving."

I glance toward Garrett, who gives me a nod of encouragement.

Focusing on my Dad again, I say, "Look, I brought you here because I wanted to tell you I'm opening my bookstore, but I also wanted to tell you that I'm no longer going to be at your and Meredith's beck and call."

Frowning, Dad replies, "What are you talking about?"

"I'm not going to be your free babysitter anymore," I explain. "I love my siblings and I'll always be there for them, but it's not my job to raise them or care for them, it's yours and

Meredith's. I'm going to have my own baby to look after, plus this business. It's been a long time since I actually lived my life. A long time since I dropped everything at a moment's notice to cater to your every need."

Dad appears stunned for several moments, staring at me with his jaw dropped.

At length, he sputters, "You're being ridiculous, Marie. Family helps each other. That's just how it is..."

"No, Dad," I sigh. "That's not how it is. You and Meredith don't treat me like family. Not really. You drop the kids on me with no consideration for my feelings or plans, and then you exclude me from family events like I don't belong at them."

Furrowing his brow, he says, "Exclude you? How do we exclude you? You always make some excuse not to be part of things that we do."

"That's not true." A part of me is relieved that he seems confused. Maybe keeping me out of things hasn't been his idea. "The twins' birthday? I didn't even know it was happening until after the fact. Their soccer and baseball games? Ballet and music recitals? Holidays? No one bothers to tell me about these things, and if I do find out about them, Meredith makes it very clear that I'm not welcome."

Dad's eyes go wide and he stares at me for several moments before murmuring, "That's...that's not true. Meredith wouldn't do that."

"She does it all the time." I let out a long breath and take a moment to gather the strength to say what I've needed to say to him for years. "Look, Dad, I'm glad you were able to find someone new after Mom. That you were able to keep living your life and build a family...I just wish you would have included me in it."

"Marie, you're my daughter." The irritation has left Dad's voice and a look of desperation passes over his face. "I never meant for you to be excluded...it...it's just when your mom died, I didn't know if I could go on without her. When I met Meredith, I was so happy and didn't want to do anything to risk the life I could have with her." He pauses and appears thoughtful for a moment before he shakes his head and softly says, "Maybe... maybe I did exclude you without realizing it. You just remind me of your mother so much, and every time I see you...it hurts."

His words are like a punch to the gut, but even as I struggle with the hurt of his realization, there's a part of me that's relieved he's finally acknowledging it. That means there might actually be hope of fixing this in time. Not today - no way in hell - but eventually, if he's willing to keep his eyes open.

"I know losing Mom was devastating," I tell him. "I know it changed everything for you, but you turned your back on me for Meredith and the kids. When I needed you most, you weren't emotionally available to me, and you didn't want to be. That's the truth, Dad. That's what I need you to recognize now."

He doesn't say anything for several moments, instead gazing around at the worn-down interior of the store again.

"Your mother loved this place," he whispers. "She poured her heart and soul into it. Sometimes I was jealous that she spent so much time here, but I loved how happy it made her." He brings his gaze back to me and for the first time in years, I feel like he's actually seeing me. "She'd be proud that you're going to bring it back to life."

My heart twists and tears form in my eyes. I swallow the lump of emotion rising up in my throat. Dad never talks about Mom.

That little bit of hope inside me grows.

"I feel her here," I confess. "More than anywhere else. I think by opening this place up again, I'll be able to hold onto her more than I have before."

Dad gulps and nods, dropping his gaze from mine again.

Clearing his throat, he says, "I...I need to go, but let's talk more about this soon, okay? I...I want to make this right somehow, Marie. I don't know how to do that right now, but I promise I'll...I'll try."

Honestly, that's more than I was expecting.

"Okay," I tell him softly. "I'd appreciate that."

He clears his throat again and fidgets awkwardly, moving from one foot to the next so he's swaying slightly.

"Good bye," he murmurs before hurrying toward the door and making his way outside. I watch him leave, and once he's gone, I feel like I can breathe again.

"You okay?" Garrett asks, moving to stand beside me and placing his hand on my back.

I give him a tired smile and nod. "Yeah, I am. Thank you for being here...and for letting me handle it. I know that wasn't easy for you."

He lets out a dry chuckle. "An understatement, but I'm proud of you for standing up to him. He needed to hear all that."

I wrap my arms around his waist and hug him, pressing my face into his chest.

"I needed to say it."

If it weren't for Garrett, I'd never have been able to stand up to my dad like that. With everything that's happened between me and Garrett, I've found the courage to use my voice. Now that I have him by my side, even when he's silent and lets me take the lead, knowing he's there and has my back makes me more determined than ever to not let anyone take me for granted every again.

He envelopes me in his strong arms and I feel warm and safe. "Do you feel better?"

"I do, actually. We have a long way to go, but I feel better about things with my Dad than I have in a long time."

Garrett drops a kiss to the top of my head. "Come on. Let's get you back home."

"Yes please."

We slip from our embrace and he grabs my hand to lead me out of the shop, never letting go as we make our way back to my house.

"FUCK, MARIE...THAT FEELS SO GOOD..."

I shiver when Garrett groans and I take his cock in deeper into my mouth.

He's sitting on the edge of my bed, and I'm on my knees on the floor, naked and already soaking wet. I want to make him feel good, though. I'm so grateful for his support today, and I want to give him as much pleasure as I possibly can.

His fingers flex around the back of my head and he pushes me to take more of him. I gag and drag my nails down his thighs, but I'm not trying to get away. This is turning me on so much, I feel like I'm going to burst with desire.

When he loosens his grip, I lift my head off him with a gasp and look back up at him. His green eyes are hooded and his cheeks flushed.

"I can't wait any longer," he growls. "I need to be inside you right fucking now."

He stands and pulls me to my feet. Spinning us around, he bends me over so I'm face down on the mattress while still standing on the floor. Taking hold of my hips, he lines himself up with my entrance and plunges into me with a single thrust.

I cry out, arching my back as pleasure explodes through me.

"Fuck, you feel so good," he snarls as he begins to pound into me from behind.

"Garrett!" I moan, grinding my hips back against him. He's

so big, and stretches me just right. It's like our bodies were made to fit together…like we were always meant to be, just like I thought.

He moves his hips faster and harder, pressing me into the mattress as he bends over to cover me with his body. Pushing my hair to the side, he kisses along my neck as he grabs my wrists and pins my arms above my head.

"You're so hot and tight," he growls into my ear. "So damn perfect. I'm going to cum inside you, baby. Do you want that?"

"Yes," I gasp. "I want it."

My clit is grinding against the bed and I feel my orgasm start to build as he drives into me mercilessly.

"I love you, Marie," he hisses. "I fucking love you so much."

"I love you too," I whimper and then my orgasm hits me so hard, I see stars. Throwing my head back, I scream as pleasure crashes through me in waves.

"Fuck!" Garrett bellows before shoving into me one final time and pouring his cum deep inside me, just like he said he would.

My orgasm goes one for several moments before I finally start to come down from the high, and my body is left in a shivering, jelly-like mess.

Panting, I slump against the bed as Garrett carefully pulls out of me.

"You okay?" he asks with a breathless chuckle.

"Fantastic," I reply, my voice muffled by the bedding my face is buried in. "I just need a moment to get the feeling back in my legs."

He laughs and I hear him walk away and into the bathroom. A few moments later, he comes back and I groan when he presses a warm, damp wash cloth between my legs and gently cleans me. When he's done, he helps me slide up into the middle of the bed before he climbs in after me. Wrapping his arms around my waist, he tucks me into his side so my head is resting on his chest.

Garrett slowly rubs my back and kisses my forehead.

"You must be exhausted," he murmurs. "Go on and sleep."

I turn my eyes up to his and ask, "Are you staying?"

It's been a little over two weeks since we became a couple, and Garrett has all but moved in already, but I still ask him if he'll stay...mostly because I like hearing his answer.

"Of course." He grins. "I'm not going anywhere, sweetheart. Not now, and not ever."

Smiling, I cuddle closer to him and breathe in his woodsy scent. Surrounded by his warmth and strength, I relax, my mind and body totally content and satisfied by this man. My White Knight.

My dream came true.

EPILOGUE

MARIE

THREE MONTHS LATER

The smell of fresh paint and sawdust still lingers in the air, mingling with the faint scent of new books. My fingers brush over the polished edge of a wooden shelf, my other hand instinctively resting on the swell of my belly. The baby gives a soft kick in response, as if sensing my excitement.

Garrett walks beside me, a clipboard in his hand, checking off items as we move through the store, his brow furrowed in concentration.

I stop in front of the cozy reading nook, where the chairs we picked out together sit with the soft lighting above them from decorative lamps. The warm glow spills across the floor, creating an inviting oasis. I sink into one of the chairs

"Perfect," I say, looking up at Garrett with a smile.

He grins, setting the clipboard aside and crouching beside me. "I told you it'd be perfect. You had the vision; I just followed orders."

I laugh softly, reaching out to brush my fingers against his cheek. "You didn't just follow orders, Garrett. You made all of this happen."

He presses a kiss to my hand before standing and helping me to my feet. "We made it happen."

As we walk toward the children's corner, my eyes are drawn to the colorful murals on the walls—vibrant scenes of storybook characters like Little Red Riding Hood and Alice in Wonderland. I imagine the sound of little feet scurrying across the soft rug, the excited chatter of kids exploring the shelves.

Garrett chuckles beside me. "What's that look for?" he asks, his tone teasing.

I smile, leaning into him as we walk. "Just imagining how much my mom would've loved this. She always dreamed of creating a place where people could escape into a story. I think we've done that."

He wraps his arm around my shoulders, pulling me close. "We have, and we're just getting started."

We step into the café area, where the counters gleam under the overhead lights. I picture the tables filled with customers sipping coffee and chatting, the smell of pastries filling the air.

"Are you nervous about the opening?" Garrett asks, his voice soft.

"A little," I admit, rubbing my belly absently. "But mostly, I'm excited. It feels like everything's finally falling into place."

We stop in the center of the store, and I take a slow turn, letting my eyes sweep over the space. Every detail has been carefully considered, from the layout of the shelves to the placement of the lighting fixtures. It's a labor of love, a testament to what we've built—not just the store, but our life together.

And what a beautiful life it is. We have each other, our friends, Garrett's family...and even mine. Things between me and Dad aren't perfect, not by a long shot, but he's been making an effort these past few months to mend our relationship.

Reaching out just to ask about my day rather than demand a favor, standing up to Meredith for me...little by little, he's showing that he genuinely cares.

"I was thinking," Garrett says, his voice pulling me back to the present. "We should name the baby something bookish since we finally got together because you helped me with my English course. Like Atticus or Matilda."

I laugh, shaking my head. "You're not naming our child Atticus."

He grins. "Fine, but I'm putting it on the table. Just in case."

I roll my eyes but can't help smiling. "We'll see."

The baby kicks softly, and I press my hand to my belly, smiling at the tiny reminder of the life growing inside me. My thoughts drift to the days ahead, imagining late-night feedings, soft coos, and the weight of our child in my arms. I think about our niece, Leila, and our nephew Oliver and how they've both filled our lives with so much joy lately. Having them around has only deepened my anticipation for our little one.

"I was thinking," I start, turning to share my thoughts, but the words catch in my throat.

Garrett isn't beside me anymore. He's behind me, kneeling on one knee.

I can't move. Time seems to slow, and the world narrows to the sight of him looking up at me, his eyes filled with love and a hint of nervousness. In his hand, he holds a small ring box. The light catches the delicate band, making it shimmer.

"Marie," he begins, his voice steady despite the weight of the moment. "I've loved you for as long as I can remember, and I know I've been slow to acknowledge it, to show it, and to say it the way I should have. Every second with you, though—every dream we've shared, every challenge we've faced—it's made me certain of one thing."

He pauses, taking a deep breath, and I realize I've stopped breathing altogether.

"I want to spend the rest of my life with you. I want to be the one you lean on, the one who makes you laugh, the one who stands beside you through everything. I want to be your husband, and I want us to be a family in every way."

Tears blur my vision as his words wash over me, filling every corner of my heart.

"Marie," he says softly, opening the box to reveal the most beautiful ring I've ever seen, "will you marry me?"

"Yes." The word escapes my lips before I can even think. My voice trembles, but there's no hesitation in my answer. "Yes, Garrett. I will absolutely marry you."

His face breaks into a smile—one of those rare, unguarded smiles that makes my knees feel weak. He takes my hand gently, slipping the ring onto my finger. It fits perfectly.

Standing, he pulls me into his arms, holding me tightly.

"I love you," I whisper against his chest, my voice muffled.

"I love you too," he murmurs, pressing a kiss to the top of my head.

As we stand there, wrapped in each other's arms, the bookstore fades into the background. All I can feel is the overwhelming sense of gratitude and excitement for what's to come—for our child, our marriage, and the life we'll build together.

We've come so far, overcome so many misunderstandings and so much hurt, but it's all brought us to this moment. I like to imagine Leila is looking down on us, smiling, happy that we are together and so in love...and proud of Garrett for keeping his promise in the end.

Want to know Christian and Haven's story?
Turn the page for a sneak peek of Fake To Forever!

ABOUT FAKE TO FOREVER

Fake marriage. Real trouble.

Christian Tallow just strolled into town with his adorable son—who also happens to be in my kindergarten class—and turned my world upside down. He's tall, broody, and basically the hero from my favorite romance novel, brought to life.

He needs a wife on paper to win his custody battle. I need to fulfill my dying mother's last wish: seeing me walk down the aisle.

Simple, right? Say "I do," keep it strictly business, and make both our problems go away. Except nothing is ever simple—especially not when you start falling for your fake husband's midnight smiles and protective streak.

Now I'm wearing a ring for all the wrong reasons, pretending my heart isn't flipping every time he says my name. If only I could remind myself it's all for show... before pretending feels way too real.

Because the only thing more dangerous than a fake marriage?
Letting your heart forget it's fake.

CHAPTER ONE: OIL RIGS AND DYING MOTHERS

HAVEN

"So... what did the doctor say today?"

The question causes me to flinch. I'd anticipated it, of course, but I hate having to answer. Releasing a long sigh, I look up to meet my brother's dark green gaze. The last thing any of us want to deal with is our mother dying. But unfortunately, that's the cards we've been dealt.

"He said it was just a matter of time now," I murmur, clutching my glass of beer so hard, my fingers turn white. "All we can do is make mom as comfortable as possible."

Garrett, who was named after our grandfather but our mother calls him Gary even though he hates it, sucks in a deep breath and lets out a long sigh before taking a drink. "I was afraid of that."

Taking a moment I try to collect my thoughts, rolling over what steps are going to be taken next. "I know you have to leave soon, but there's a chance she won't be here when you get back."

He nods, his scruffy jaw tensing at my words. "Yeah, I figured as much. There isn't much that I can do though right now. They'll let me come back early, if something happens."

At least there's that.

I lift my head higher and reach out to snag his arm in my hand, unable to hold back my relief. "I didn't think the oil fields would be that flexible for you."

"It'd be different if I was on an off-shore rig, but since I'm inland, it's easier."

Thank fuck for that.

I feel like a bit of the weight on my shoulders has been lifted. His boss acts like the rest of the world doesn't exist outside of the oil fields when Garrett's out there, so I've been scared he wouldn't let my brother go if things with Mom took a turn while he was away. Though, the doctor said that in cases like this, it could be months before... before it takes her.

At least, that was the case for other patients.

"How's Peter doing?" Garrett asks, pulling me from my thoughts.

Peter, our stepfather, is so over the moon in love with our mom. I know her death will devastate him. I don't want to put any more stress on Garrett's shoulders, so I don't tell him how Peter barely kept it together after the doctor gave Mom's final prognosis.

"As good as can be expected, I guess. Losing Mom is obviously going to be hard for him, but he was putting on a brave front today."

"Peter's a good guy." Garrett shrugs, dropping his gaze from mine. "He's always been good. You've always been good too, Haven. You're better than me, especially when it comes to Mom. I know I should've been there today, but I just... you know..."

I do know.

Reaching out to squeeze his arm, I try to offer what comfort I can. "Don't worry, I get it. It's a lot, but you promise you'll see Mom before you leave, right?"

"Of course." His voice trembles. It's barely discernible, but I pick up on it. I know him too well. It's hard for him to see Mom suffering. Garrett's the type of guy who sees a problem and wants to fix it, but he can't fix Mom. He's also not good at dealing with feelings of helplessness. "I just didn't want to be there and listen to the doctor tell us there wasn't any more hope. I want to believe something can be done."

We fall into silence as we drink. What more is there to say, really? Even though I'm on the verge of tears, I hold them back. Crying never solved anything, and I don't want to make Garrett feel worse than he already does. If I can focus on the soft murmur of the bar's activities around me, I can hold out and delay my breakdown until later, when I'm alone and away from my brother.

Besides, I can't let my emotions ruin our time together. It's tradition that before Garrett goes off for his month-long shift in the nearby oil fields, we come to our favorite spot, *Carson's*, and sit at the bar together to get drunk before he goes off to join his fellow *roughnecks*.

A term that some like, and others detest.

Living in Blue Ridge, Texas, roughnecks are everywhere. Plenty of oil magnates reside in this state, and some even come from the off-shore rigs in the Gulf, working inland until the more work off-shore opens up for them.

Roughnecks, for the most part, are younger, wiry guys with muscular forearms, tattoos, and sometimes less than spotless backgrounds. My giant of a brother fits that description to a T, apart from the shady past. He towers over me with his 6'2" height and wide, muscular frame. His dark hair and closely cropped beard give him a rugged appearance, and he has a reputation for being a total playboy, since the girls seem to throw themselves at him.

Which is the last thing I ever want to think about.

It's absolutely disgusting to watch. Not to mention, desperation never looked good on anyone.

Garrett finishes his beer and then waves the bartender, a burly man who looks more like a lumberjack than a bartender, over to order another one.

"Did I tell you my friend Christian is moving into town?"

The topic change is abrupt, but I get it. He is trying to push our current situation to the back of his mind to lighten the mood.

"Your friend from college? The billionaire?" I scoff, raising a brow as I turn my gaze to him. "Why the hell would he move to Blue Ridge?"

"He wants a quieter life, I guess." Garrett shrugs. "The peaceful small town experience, you know?"

I can't help but roll my eyes. "Ah, I gotcha. Isn't that what most people want by moving to Texas?"

He chuckles at my comment, shaking his head. "They think so."

What Garrett really means is his rich buddy decided he wants to come to our town, build a monstrosity of a house that he'll call his 'country home,' and spend a couple weekends out of the year here when he gets bored with the city. Typical.

Garrett absentmindedly scratches at the stubble on his cheek. "Anyways, he's coming to town next week. I'll be in the fields by then, but once I'm back, I want you two to finally meet."

Finally meet? Oh joy.

"Oh, yeah?" I chuckle. "Don't tell me you're going to try and hook me up with your rich, pretentious middle-aged friend, Garrett. I've already told you, I'm not..."

"I'm not trying to hook you up with anyone," he insists. I know him better than that, and it's not like this wouldn't be the first time.

"Right… so you're telling me you just want us to meet for shits and giggles?"

Garrett nods to the bartender when his beer is placed in front of him, frowning at me before he takes a drink. "I promise you, I've no intention of hooking you two up… and he's not middle-aged. He's just a guy, and he's not going to hit on you, so you don't need to worry about that."

"Good. Because I'm not looking to date any stuck-up oil magnate nepo baby."

"You have such a weird thing against rich people," Garrett mutters, causing my mouth to drop open.

"It's not weird! We grew up with practically nothing. People like your friend are born with a silver spoon in their mouths, and they don't appreciate anything."

Garrett's back stiffens at my words, his eyes refusing to meet mine. "Christian's worked hard for what he has."

I know Garrett's just defending his friend, but I refuse to back down. "How hard do you have to work if daddy gives you your first job?"

Never one to let things bother him for too long, Garrett takes another swig of his beer, shaking his head. "I guess we'll just have to agree to disagree."

I scowl at him, playing with the little bowl of peanuts between us. Finding the biggest one, I chuck it at his head, and laugh when it bounces off and lands in his beard. Garrett's always taken care of me, and been the best big brother anyone could ask for. Growing up poor in a small town like Blue Ridge was hard, but Garrett made sure I always had what I needed, and even a few things I wanted by taking extra shifts or working odd jobs. That was before he became head honcho of the inland rig just north of Blue Ridge.

Maybe he's a little overprotective, but he's a good big brother.

Not that I'm going to tell him that. He has a big enough head already.

Suppose I should trust his judgment when it comes to his friends. I don't really understand why or how he became friends with the likes of Christian Tallow to begin with—outside of them both going to the same college. Tallow is a billionaire oil tycoon who could not have grown up more differently from us. We worked our asses off just to get by, and Tallow came from a wealthy family who helped him build his own massive wealth.

The bar's front door opens and a group of four guys come inside, talking and laughing loudly. I spare them a glance, but that's about it. Since half the town works on the rigs, it's a safe assumption they're roughnecks. They make their way toward the pool tables on the other side of the bar, and I turn back to Garrett. He's watching me with an arched brow and a small grin playing around his lips.

"What?" I demand to know, frowning. "Why are you looking at me like that?"

"You want to go talk to those guys?" A smirk plays behind the lip of his beer.

"That is such a weird thing for you to say." I turn back around on my stool, effectively tuning the group out. Definitely not interested. "You know, older brothers usually don't want their sisters to date."

"Is it so wrong for me to want to see my baby sister settled and happy? To actually go out with a guy and have a little fun once in a while?"

"I appreciate your concern, Garrett, but I'm fine. I don't need anyone right now. Between work and taking care of Mom, I'm too busy."

The look he sends my way tells me he's not letting this go anytime soon. And I have a feeling I'm not going to like what he says next.

"What are you going to do when Mom isn't around anymore?"

The question makes my stomach twist so hard, bile rises up my throat, but I manage to swallow it back down and push away the fear and pain that his words provoke.

"I'll figure it out," I say, my words weak even to my own ears. "I'm an adult, Garrett, who can manage her life on my own."

"But you shouldn't have to." He slams his bottle down with a little more force than needed, causing a few peanuts to fall out of the bowl. "You should have a family of your own and a life outside of our family's tiny bubble. It's what you've always wanted."

Perhaps, but we don't always get what we want, do we?

"Look who's talking," I reply, slapping on a grin to hide the effect what he's saying is having on me. "Am I really getting this lecture from my workaholic brother who gets bored with a girl so quickly, she doesn't last more than a couple of dates?"

"Yeah, well, I'm not exactly the family type," he says. He looks away, a shadow falling over his eyes, but I'm too fired up to deal with his own insecurities.

"You do realize how hypocritical that is, right?"

Garrett grumbles under his breath before replying, "Whatever. I just worry about you, okay? I know Mom worries too. We just don't want you to be lonely."

I appreciate his concern, I really do. But I'm not a little kid anymore, and now's not the time for me to be thinking about shit like that. He'll be leaving soon, and there's no point spending what little time we have left arguing.

"Don't worry about me. I'm fine. I'm very happy with my life, and if I decide someday that I want the whole marriage, kids, and white picket fence, I'll make it happen."

Garrett smirks and shakes his head. "You make it sound so

easy, but I know you, Haven. If you do decide to give your heart to someone, he's going to have to be someone extraordinary. Someone who isn't from Blue Ridge. The world is much bigger than this place, and you belong out in it."

His words warm my heart, but I don't let him know that. I lift my glass to take a long drink, not wanting Garrett to see the effect his statement is having on me. He's right. The world is much bigger than Blue Ridge, but this town is what I know and where I feel safe. It's where my family is.

Venturing outside of Blue Ridge would open me up to all the heartbreak and dangers the rest of the world holds. I've experienced enough pain in my life already, and I'm not interested in going out and inviting more in.

Blue Ridge is where I belong, and I just need to keep on focusing on the things that matter most to me so that I don't lose them. My family, my friends, and my job. I don't need more than that. Garrett might not get it, even if I fully explained it to him, and that's okay. I don't need him to understand. I just need him to come back from the oil fields safe and sound.

If I can maintain what I already have and the people I already care about, I'll never have to let anyone else in... which also means I won't have to worry about losing anyone else either.

Want to know what happens next?

Scan the QR code below to continue reading Fake To Forever!

ABOUT THE AUTHOR

Subscribe to my newsletter to stay up to date on all things Noelle Stone!

Follow me on social media and join my Facebook group for sneak peeks into what's coming next!

AUTHOR BIO:

She's the literary architect of dashing billionaires and sassy, sweet heroines, adding heart-pounding twists and turns to every tale.

Her castle is filled with her loyal husband and the feline rockstar, Freddie Mercury Jr.

When she's not conjuring love stories, you'll catch her conquering the waves with her dragon boat crew, turning every adventure into a page-turner!